Soul Seeks the Truth

Fizza Younis

Dedicated to all the lost souls,
Roaming the world without purpose,
Floating through life without reason,
Waiting to be found.

Contents

Foreword

Sometimes, words aren't just words, but rather a mirror to your soul. And souls can be both dark and angelic. Regardless, they all seek one thing: *the truth* —about the universe, life, and most importantly, about themselves.

I have always believed in the truth. It's the only important thing in this world. Unfortunately, it's never simple because it has many faces. It wears many masks. And it isn't always visible to the naked eye. Those who seek it tend to find it sooner or later.

Sometimes, it chooses to reveal itself to the unsuspecting souls as well, and in the process, changes their lives. Change isn't always for the best, though. So, let's hope when the truth reveals itself to us, we are strong enough and determined enough to change for the better and not for the worse.

I often think about random things. I'm sure it will be evident from my work. That's how these stories came to be: too much free time and too many things to think about. My mind refused to take a break, and my thoughts needed an outlet. This is how I feel connected. I wrote these stories over the past year and decided to share them with the world.

Because art, in any form or shape, is meant to be shared.

These stories needed to be told, and I have told them. What I have written and what you will read might not be the same. Even though I like these stories, you might hate them. But even if you do, know this: not everything is meant to be liked. Some things only need to be felt.

In any case, I do hope that you enjoy stories about lost *souls seeking the truth*.

Souls Don't Tell Lies

It was one of those lazy Sunday mornings that could transport you to your past. Lately, certain things weighed on my mind, and I was getting restless. Since I had nowhere to be, no one to see, and nothing important to do, I decided to go out. I went to visit my favorite café and read for a while. After all, what better way to relax and rejuvenate? Or so I had thought.

That was when it happened. In a single moment, my perception of life changed drastically. I felt the need to be more than who I was, more than an ordinary person living a very conventional and mundane life. I hated the change. I feared it even. I was scared of leaving my comfort zone. Cocooned in my neatly organized principled life, I wasn't ready to admit that basically, I was a coward.

Reading was my escape. It was something that made me feel brave. Between the pages of a book, I could almost pretend to be an adventurer. It felt right somehow. There was no need for me to be a risk-taker. Why would I want to when I could keep living a peaceful, albeit boring life? That day, everything changed when I received a note from a stranger.

There I was, minding my business and reading one of my all-time favorite books when someone passed me a note. I opened it. "Are you happy?" That was all it said, no names or anything else.

It was a simple question that someone who cared for you might ask. Was I happy? I thought I was until that very moment. All at once, I wasn't so sure. What was happiness anyway? Do we even know that? I was living a quiet life with a job, a house, and something to read at any time. I always thought that was enough. But was it?

Even now, I'm uncertain why I responded to that one question the way I did. I wasn't that person. I was never the one to listen to my heart. My brain had always been the dominant organ until that fine, fateful day. Perhaps it was someone else who took over my consciousness. At least, that is the only plausible explanation I can find. But then words have undeniable power. We all know this, especially those of us who read as we breathe.

So, back to that day. After reading the cryptic note, I looked around searching for its author. It wasn't a question you would ask a stranger, so I wondered who wrote it and why would they be interested in my happiness. That was when our eyes met. It was the first time I noticed how mesmerizingly warm the brown color could be. Little did I know that those eyes would haunt me for the rest of my life.

The woman stood up and walked towards me. "May I sit here?" She whispered, or maybe she had one of those husky voices that sounded like a whisper.

"Yes, sure. Do I know you?" I replied, posing a question of my own.

"I doubt it, but I know you. I've known you for as long as I've known myself," she said. She sounded like a creepy stalker. It was bizarre, but I stayed quiet. I waited for her to elaborate and wasn't disappointed when she continued. "This may come as a surprise to you. We are soul twins."

"Okay?" I wasn't sure how to respond to that statement. What was *soul twins* anyway?

I was beginning to fear that I had made a big mistake talking to a stranger. I was never a big conversationalist. It wasn't normal for me to talk to strangers. I sometimes wonder why I welcomed the woman's company. I still don't have an answer to that question. All I can say is that something about her felt right. I didn't know her. At the same time, I believed it when she said that she knew me.

"I can see your skepticism. I assure you I'm no looney. I know what I'm talking about. We were meant to meet like this. I've waited a long time for this very moment. There is so much I need to say. And so much you should understand before we start our journey together." She looked at me as if I were the most precious thing in the world.

It should've been weird, and yet it wasn't. I was listening to her as if my very existence depended on it. Still, I wasn't someone to throw caution away completely.

"Look, lady, I have no idea who you are and what you are talking about. Either explain yourself in a way I can comprehend or kindly leave me to my reading."

The woman was undeterred.

"There is no reason for you to get annoyed, Sarah. All in good time," she said with a smile, "let me explain, please."

She had called me by my name. I was now sure that she was a stalker. She might have frequented the same café. It wasn't like I noticed people or my surroundings.

"You do know me," I stated. "How? What do you want from me?"

"Nothing more than your time," she said in a calm monotone. "First, answer my question. Are you happy?"

"Yes and no. I'm not sure. I'm content, I think."

"No, that's not what I meant, dear, or rather it isn't what I want to hear from you. You cannot live life like this. It isn't living. You exist and nothing more. You need to be happy. I wish to see you laugh out loud. I wish you to feel exhilarated by something you are passionate about. What are you passionate about?"

This conversation was spiraling out of control. Who was she, and how did she know about my life? True I had never thought of my life as boring, but she had a point. I was living a half-hearted life. It sounded depressing coming from someone else's mouth. I was at peace. Wasn't I? I didn't need passion or laughter. I preferred my quiet existence.

Once again, I was lost for words. My confusion was palpable. That woman had the wheels of my thoughts churning. The first thing was first, though. "I'm not sure why you're asking me this. Why are you interested in my life?" I asked.

"Did I not tell you that I am your soul twin? Of course, I'm interested in your life, in you," she replied in her calm manner, which I was beginning to associate with her. She had an air of tranquility, which was very soothing, albeit hard to decipher. I wanted her to keep talking. "If you're happy, I'll keep living as I always have. Your unhappiness will lead to turbulence in my life." Now she sounded sad.

I laughed at that. You might not understand the importance of it, but I laughed! I never laughed. I smiled. Full-on laughter was so unlike me, but I couldn't help it. I was beginning to think she was indeed a looney. Also, I wondered why I was listening to her aptly. She had me intrigued, I would give her that. I was curious to know more if there was more.

"So, let me get this straight. You think our souls

are twins and my happiness is related to yours. Is that right?"

"Yes, that's correct except I don't think it. I know it for a fact." She smiled again.

"That's absurd. Besides, I've told you I'm quite content with my life. Thank you!" I was getting impatient as the conversation entered unchartered territory, making me uncomfortable.

Who talked about *souls* and *happiness*? Those things didn't mean anything in this paper world. She was making me think about things I'd rather not think about.

"Please, listen to me! You can't live like this forever. You must find your passion and pursue it. You need to be happy. It's of utmost importance," she said earnestly.

"Okay, tell me more," I said, even though I didn't want to listen to her anymore. Yet, I also wanted to see where she was going with her unusual demands.

"Every soul is created in twos, like ours. Two souls come into existence together. One is destined to be born into this world, while the other remains unbound and free to roam the universe. It exists without actually existing. When its twin dies, both souls return to their origin and become one. Our souls have existed for over a hundred years, and then you were born as Sarah, and I remained unbound. It was a happy existence for me until you started to wither away. I can't stand by and watch you waste this life. You must take full advantage of what has been given to you so that when you return to your origin and the two of us become one, there are no regrets or unfulfilled dreams and no desire to get another chance because this is it. We will not get another chance ever again." She was trying to explain things in a way she thought I would understand.

She was wrong because nothing she said made any sense to me. It was all so farfetched that it sounded like a plot of a science fiction novel. "You are right in front of me, and you want me to believe you are a soul without a body? Are you serious?" I pointed out the most obvious flaw in her theory.

"I can explain that." She kept smiling, and now her smile was starting to creep me out. Her eyes remained the same, warm and inviting. "I'm not here, nor are we having this conversation. At least not in a way that humans do, but it's our souls conversing with each other."

"That's ridiculous! I'm here, in my favorite café, reading what I love the most. You wrote me a note, a note! That's as human as you can get." I was a little more forceful with my statements than I needed to be but it was the last straw. Now, she wanted me to believe that I was hallucinating.

Had my life become so pointless that I was having conversations with my *soul twin?* The thought was very disturbing. Immediately, I started to think about the last time I had a real conversation with someone who wasn't a character from one of my favorite books. I was turning into a pitiful creature. No wonder my so-called *soul twin* was worried about my very existence.

Huh, I was starting to believe her. My logical and rational mind was telling me to trust her beautiful brown eyes. They said, 'eyes didn't lie,' and hers seemed honest. But how could I believe in things like *soul twins?* No, I couldn't. No matter how trustworthy her eyes were, her words were fiction. Or so I thought until someone was shaking me awake.

I had fallen asleep while reading, and when I woke up, there was no woman with warm brown eyes anywhere in the café. There was no note inquiring about my happiness. It was me and my book, as usual—just us. But I was left with a nagging feeling in my gut, those hauntingly pretty eyes in my mind, and that soothing husky voice in my ears, urging me to be happy, to be passionate, and to live my life to the fullest because it was the only one that I had got. I knew then it was no mere dream. I had finally found the courage to seek my adventure and that altered the course of my life forever, thanks to my soul twin.

Wherever she is right now, I'm sure she is still smiling at me.

Deafening Silence

I was lost for a long time. I guess that's how most of us feel when we search for a purpose in this world of chaos and constant disruptions. Sometimes, we accept our existence on this planet and everything it entails as it is, while most of the time, we seek to change things. Some of us live well, while others struggle every minute of every day. Some seek a higher meaning in life, wanting to be more and to do more, while others drift through the stream of life without direction.

I was among the latter and didn't believe in seeking the purpose of life. I believed no one could ever really know what that purpose was, so why bother? I lived one day at a time. There wasn't much I wanted from life except a peaceful death. I hoped to go to bed one day and never wake up again. At least, that's what I thought until the day my life came unhinged.

That day started like any other. There was nothing special about it. I woke up like I always did and went to work as usual. I was a pharmacist whose professional life was as mundane as it could be.

"You lack ambition, Hansel," my sister would say.

"I'm content with everything I have," I would reply.

I had nothing to prove to anyone, least of all to myself. So, I never strived to be better. I was an average person living an average life, doing what most people did. My sister's approval wasn't something I sought.

That day, however, was a turning point for me. After work, I decided to visit my sister. That was something out of the norm for me because I wasn't close to her. Also, living in different cities made it difficult to run into each other. I even made a point of avoiding her if I could help it.

Farah was my only living family, the only person I loved and resented at the same time. She was my opposite. She was everything I wasn't. She thought being older gave her a right to nag me about everything from my career to my lack of love life. That was probably the reason I avoided seeing her.

She was a doctor come actress. She pursued the field of medicine and then decided that wasn't what she wanted. Good for her, not so much for the patients who relied on her. Regardless, whatever she did, she did it well. She was a brilliant doctor, and now her acting skills were unmatched. If I were truthful, I'd admit I admired her, but I wasn't that honest.

When I saw her, Farah was very happy, which wasn't so unusual for her. She was a happy person, happier than most.

"You look excited about something," I said.

"Well, it's a surprise. You'd know when the time's right," she said without giving me any details. I hated it when she did that. She could be so dramatic at times, and she loved creating suspense. I was sure it was nothing special and didn't press the point. Even a new dress or a pair of shoes she liked could make her happy.

"Sure," I said, and changed the subject, "How have you been?"

"I'm fine. Now that you finally got the time to visit your sister," she said in a way that made me feel guilty as if I had done something wrong.

"I've been busy," I replied, inwardly telling myself she didn't visit me either, and I was guilty of nothing.

"Yeah, as if," she smiled, teasing me. "I'm your sister, remember? I know you well, and I also know how busy you are not." She had no clue, but she liked to pretend otherwise.

I shrugged and thought it better not to argue with her. "I missed you and wanted to spend some time with you."

"As you can see, never been better." She gave me her best smile. She was the kind of person who could brighten up even the darkest corners. "You don't seem well." She was also very perceptive, even though not many would guess that about her.

"I'm fine," I had no idea how to explain it to her, "I just…"

"You need someone to make you happy." Once again, she reminded me that my reclusive lifestyle was no way to live. "You aren't happy, and I'm not living in the same city to visit you often. I worry for you. You've mourned for long enough. Don't you think?" She had to go there.

"That has nothing to do with it. I'm just never happy. That doesn't mean that I'm sad," I replied. "I'm content with my life. There is nothing wrong with that. You know I'm not an emotional person. I don't think I can ever feel truly happy anyway."

Sometimes, I wondered if there was something wrong with me. I'd never voice my fears in front of anyone, least of all my sister. My lack of emotions made it difficult for me to get attached to others. I didn't even have any close friends. Most people I knew kept their distance from me. That was wise, though. People only complicated things, and I needed a drama-free life.

"Still, you need to start living a little," she persisted.

"People die, so why get attached to someone only to mourn their absence later," I said at last.

"You don't love because you fear loss?" She sounded shocked.

It was probably the most revealing conversation I had had with her. I didn't know why I said it. It wasn't unusual for her to criticize my lifestyle. I had never tried to explain it to her before. She wouldn't understand, and I wasn't the type to give explanations.

I admired my sister's strength. She dealt with loss well. She knew how precious life was, and she also knew how fragile it was. She had somehow found her balance. While I was lost, more now than ever before.

We talked some more, and then I left. On my way back home, my car was hit by a truck. I lost consciousness on the impact. I didn't remember feeling any pain. One minute, I was thinking about my sister's blissful life, and the next minute, it was all dark and silent.

I remembered the silence. That's all I could recall. It was profound. Don't worry, I didn't die that day. I just went to hell. At least I wasn't lost anymore. I finally knew where I was, but I still didn't know why I ended up there.

I woke up deaf. I couldn't hear a single sound, not that there was any sound there. The silence reigned supreme. All was quiet. I couldn't even hear my voice.

It was a strange place. As far as I could see, there were poppy fields, nothing else. I didn't see any roads or trails, so I walked around without direction, without purpose. I had no idea how long I wandered in those endless fields. It could've been an hour, one day, or a month. I was neither tired nor was I hungry or thirsty. However, I was frustrated and lonely.

I wanted to go home and talk to my sister some more. Maybe even move closer to her so that I would see her more often. Most of all, I wanted to hear a sound and listen to music. Any sound.

At that moment, I realized how scared I was and how terrifying the silence was. No wind blew, no birds chirped, the sun didn't set, and that one day stretched to infinity, never-ending. That's how I knew I was in hell. Because where else could it be? In the silent poppy fields, I was all alone, and there was nothing for me to do except think.

Ultimately, I accepted my fate. I sat down and contemplated. I thought about my life and about all the things I never got to do. I had never fallen in love. I didn't travel anywhere exciting. I never dreamed any dreams. Mostly, I never really lived. I merely existed.

I never did anything for anyone, never went out of my way to help another soul. It's true that I also never intentionally harmed anyone, but that's not the point. The point was that I was self-engrossed, no one else mattered, and nothing else carried weight. That was my life. Was it a good one? I thought it was better than many, but it's also true that it could've been so much more. Then I remembered...

There was a time when things were different.

Before our parents died in a senseless shooting incident, Farah and I were close, as close as any two siblings could ever be. We shared everything. We talked too much, and we laughed too hard. We were a perfect picture of a happy family.

Our parents had made sure that we knew nothing of life's worries. In those days, I also had dreams. I wanted to see the world. I wanted to find a cure for cancer. I wanted to do so many things. I was as enthusiastic about life as my sister. I loved life. I loved all the people around me.

I had no idea how I had forgotten that time of my life when the sun shone just a little bit brighter, the stars glared with a little bit more dazzle, the wind blew more strongly, and I smiled more happily. I was happy. I was!

I had no idea it was even a possibility for me. But, at that moment, I remembered my smile, my life full of merriment. "So, there was more to life after all," I thought. Among the poppies and the silence, I finally heard my heart's cries.

I realized what was missing, and my hell became my heaven. As deafening as the silence was, it made me listen to what my sister had been trying to say for a long time. Finally, I decided I wanted more. I wanted to be happy once again. Unfortunately, it wasn't meant to be. I was in hell, and there was no way out of it.

That's the last thing I thought about before I woke up from death. This time in a hospital bed.

Farah was asleep in a chair beside my bed. Seeing her face made me genuinely happy. I was back in the world of the living and promised to do better this time around. I planned to live for others.

∞ ∞ ∞

"Oh well, I almost forgot the most important part," I said, looking at the curious faces of my audience.

"What's that?" My niece asked.

I was surrounded by my family. My children, nieces, nephews, and grandchildren were all there. Everyone had come to visit me now that I was no longer able to leave the house. I was dying, and I knew that in my heart. But things were different this time around.

"That's also how I met your Aunt," I continued. "She stole my heart. It was love at first sight."

"I want to hear more about Mother," my daughter said. She loved it every time I told the story of how I met Torri in the hospital after my accident.

I had almost died, which had changed the course of my life. But sometimes, I wondered how much of it was because of my near-death experience and how much was because of Torri's love. She was a doctor who had devoted her entire life to serving humanity. She truly cared about her patients. She brought me back to life, both literally and figuratively.

"Where is she now?" My grandson, the youngest member of the family, asked. He hadn't met his grandmother. She died before he was born. To him, she was just a story.

"She is in heaven." I smiled sadly.

It was amazing how many emotions I could feel at once. I was happy that I had met Torri. I was sad that I had lost her so soon afterward. And I was hopeful that I would meet her again.

How you live your life determines where you'll end up after you die. I hoped no one ended up in a silent poppy field, and if they did, they were lucky enough to find their way back the way I did.

I was in limbo for a long time, and then suddenly I was in hell. I did end up getting another chance at life. That life, for me, was heaven, and now I had no regrets. Death was nearby. I knew that. But this time around, I wouldn't end up anywhere bad. I knew that, too.

"My Torri awaits me on the other side, not those dreadful poppies nor that deafening silence," I whispered to myself, closing my eyes and taking one last, deep breath.

Lost in Time

"The most important thing in life is to know what isn't important. It's better to let go of all the things weighing you down, especially when they don't matter. Don't let others tell you how to live your life. Ask yourself, look into your own heart because you already have all the answers you need." That was the advice my mother gave me when I was twelve.

I always listened to my mother because she knew what was best for me. She loved me more than anyone else could, and I knew she would never lead me astray. Even though she was no longer with me I still remembered everything she ever said to me.

She raised me to believe in myself and to be persistent. She always told me the importance of being decisive and never regret things that go wrong. She was a scientist like me, and we knew that life was just an experiment, a trial, and a lot could go wrong.

"Life is uncertain, sweetheart. Things can and do go awry, and that's okay. Mistakes can be corrected, and wrongs can be righted," she would often say, and like a fool, I believed her.

∞ ∞ ∞

"You're so stubborn. It's not always a good thing to take risks even if your plan seems perfect," Sandy warned me. "Sometimes, instead of going forward, it's okay to take a left or a right turn."

"I don't care what you think. I love you, but there are things you don't understand," I replied.

"We've been friends for ten years now. I know you well enough," she sighed, "You're going to do it, aren't you?"

"I must. There is no other way. The day I lost my mother was the worst day of my life. If I can turn back time and save her, I'll do it at any cost." My mind was made up.

"You're not thinking clearly." She cautioned me again.

"I've never been so sure of anything in my life. I want to do this. This is important to me." I wasn't the kind of person who changed her mind easily. Once I made a decision, I stood by it.

"Why?" she asked.

"First of all, it's something that my mother started. She invented this time machine. And somehow, I feel she must've wanted me to continue her work. Secondly, I may succeed and save her." I explained it to her as best as I could.

"Really? Have you considered that your mother had a good reason to stop working on this experiment when she did?" She pointed out.

"No, she just wasn't as stubborn as I am." I winked at her.

It was the truth though. I remembered how passionate she was about time travel. She used to talk about her theories a lot. That was why I wanted to continue it, and I wouldn't get discouraged. Besides, I was almost there. Everything had been planned to the smallest detail. I knew where I was going and what I must do once I was there. And I planned to return once my mission was complete. My mother's time machine was operative.

"I hope you don't regret it," Sandy said, sighing a little.

I was annoyed with her for being so negative. "Do you think I haven't considered the dangers involved in this venture? All the things that can go wrong? Trust me, I have. I won't regret it even if the worst happened."

With that thought in mind, I pressed the button to close the doors. The room I was in went dark. It was a small room, the size of an elevator. There were no windows but a door and mirrors on the three sides. I pressed the red button that would take me back to a time when my mother was still alive.

I wondered how my mother would feel when she found out her time machine worked. She would be so happy. It was unfortunate her life's work went to waste simply because she wasn't brave enough to continue her experiments. I was though. I was a risk taker and bet my whole existence on something no one had ever done before.

∞∞∞

"Some things are just not important, Anna." Someone was speaking in hushed tones. I vaguely recognized the voice. "It was never about courage, sweetheart. I knew when to stop. I didn't give up. Do you think my life's work was wasted? Dear girl, I invented that machine hoping to discover a way to travel in time. I knew it would work, but testing it was never important. My present was so perfect. I didn't want to go back in time to change my life. My life with you was perfect."

My head felt weird. I couldn't feel my limbs. I was hyperventilating. Something was terribly wrong. Where was I? Who was this person whispering in my ear, and what kind of gibberish were they spouting? Nothing was making any sense.

"Honey, I love you, know this. The only thing you can do now is let go of the past. Let go of me and live your life for yourself."

That's the last thing I remembered before I blacked out again.

∞∞∞

I woke up in a hospital. I had no idea how I got there. Those words someone had spoken so softly still reverberated in my mind, but they meant nothing to me. It must have been a dream.

"Anna, you're up," the lady from the church said. "They say you can return to the orphanage in a few days. Thankfully, nothing was broken."

That's when I remembered. I had fallen from the tree behind the church and hit my head on the pavement. Ah! So, that's why it hurt so much. I tried to smile at her, but it was more of a wince.

"Don't worry, you'll be good as new in no time."

∞∞∞

"What do you think happened?" Sandy asked.

"Anna went back in time and lost everything," Mrs. Stevenson replied.

"What do you mean?" Sandy didn't understand it.

"How much did you girls know about Dana's project?"

"We have been working on it for more than six years now. Anna wanted to continue her mother's experiments. We've read all of her notes and instructions. I think we know enough."

"You didn't know the most important part. Otherwise, you wouldn't have let Anna use that machine." Mrs. Stevenson looked disappointed.

"What do you mean?" Sandy was confused.

"What year did she choose to go back to?" She asked pointedly.

"2023."

"Ah! That explains it, then."

"What?" Sandy was still confused.

"She was never born." Mrs. Stevenson was being cryptic.

"What do you mean?"

"It's true that Dana's invention works, but there was a glitch in the system. You cannot go forth in time, only back, and even that has serious consequences. Anna went to 2023, you say. She was seven years old back then. So now she is a seven-year-old girl in 2023. However, not as our Anna. Our Anna is gone. She would be starting over as an entirely different person. Dana realized it during the last stages of her project and just gave up on it. To go back in time when you were alive meant that you would lose your existence and start over as someone else. Time travel is a tricky business. Too many unknowns are involved. No one can predict what kind of life they would end up having the second time around." Mrs. Stevenson explained it as simply as possible.

"You mean Anna Brown ceased to exist?" Sandy couldn't believe her ears.

"Yes."

"But if she never existed, then how come we still have memories of her?" At least, that was how time travel in fiction worked.

"We will always have these memories. We knew her in this timeline. Everyone who knew her here will remember her. Unfortunately, she won't remember any of us. She won't have any memories of her past or present. She would have very different memories. I hope that she found a better life."

"I don't think that's possible because what can be better than perfect?" Sandy said sadly.

Some things are not important and must be left alone. Just because you can, doesn't mean that you should. Anna wanted to see her mother again and even save her from death. She wanted to prove that her mother's work was worth something. In the process, she lost everything. She lost the woman she loved the most.

Most importantly, she lost herself somewhere in time, forgotten forever.

A Stranger in Town

It wasn't easy, but then it wasn't supposed to be. Nothing worthwhile in life ever came easy, at least not for him. His life was a series of unfortunate incidents, starting at the time of his birth, and still, things kept going wrong. No matter how hard he tried to be the best version of himself, people wouldn't let him be that.

Everyone was always nagging him, telling him how to live his life, criticizing him, pointing out all the things he didn't have and all the wrongs he did. Was it his fault that his mother died after giving him birth or that his father left him to see the world when he was only eleven? No, it wasn't.

He was trying to make do with what was handed to him. But no one cared for him. No one ever bothered to ask him how he was doing. People always mocked him and called him names. Life was hard enough, and he was tired. And it was time for him to say no to these toxic people in his life. He had to take control. Yet again, things were going out of control, all thanks to one nosy neighbor.

It all started when Mrs. Shelley moved in next

door to him. She was an interfering busybody, as annoying as any sixty-something-year-old woman could be. For some reason, she got an instant dislike of him. First, she had an issue with the odd timings he kept. Every time she saw him, she would let him know how unhealthy it was to sleep in. "You should rise with the sun if you want to live a long life," she would say.

He tried to be polite and ignored her as much as possible. But no, her nagging didn't end there. Then, she had an issue with him ordering pizza so often. "Eat something other than pizza if you don't want to end up in a wheelchair later in life." The woman was relentless when it came to criticizing others. Sometimes, she would advise him on how to keep his front garden, and sometimes, she would tell him to go out more, work more, blah blah... The list went on, and he tried to ignore her until he no longer could.

She wasn't the first person he killed, but she gave him the most trouble, and now he was on the run. He had planned it well, or so he had thought. However, he didn't think the old lady living alone might know a few things about keeping herself safe.

Anyway, that wasn't the end. He would start over, and everything would go back to normal. It's not like he did something bad. The woman was asking for it. She didn't deserve to live. These old folks think they knew everything about everything, as if!

Even if you had spent your life well, it didn't mean you could judge everyone else. She didn't know him. She had no idea of the things he had faced in life, of the bullies and the illness that festered in his head. Most days, staying sane was a struggle. Only if people realized that and minded their own business, then he wouldn't have to kill anyone.

Unfortunately, they made him do it. Anyone he got close to ended up being murdered. In truth, he didn't enjoy killing, but these annoying people made it impossible for him to let them live. He wasn't the villain; he was just a tragic hero forced to live a life he didn't ask for.

"Here is your order. Would you like anything else?" the waitress asked.

"No, thank you," Kevin said, forcing a smile.

He had noticed the pretty waitress, whatever her name was. Every time he came to the diner to eat, she hovered around his table more than necessary. It was so obvious she was interested in him. He had no interest in her or anyone else, for that matter. He didn't date, and letting people into his life was dangerous. That's why he lived alone.

Usually, he preferred big cities. It was easier to blend in and be invisible when there were thousands of people around you. Unfortunately, he was stuck in this small town for the moment. Dodging people wasn't easy when everyone knew everyone and wanted to know everything about them. It was such a mess. Only if he had been a little more careful. In any case, he was going to do what he did best and make do.

∞ ∞ ∞

Anna watched Kevin leave and sighed. She had fallen in love with him at first sight. The moment he walked into her dinner, it was like shooting stars and all that romantic mumbo jumbo. The point was that she was head over heels in love, but the arrogant man didn't even know she existed. Or maybe he was just extremely shy. There was no doubt that he was charismatic. She had been trying to get his attention for months but to no avail. She highly doubted he even knew her name.

That tall, dark, and mysterious stranger had been the talk of the town since the day he moved there. He was only in his early twenties, but clearly, he came from money as he had bought the Turner Mansion. At first, it was innocent curiosity about the new arrival. That wasn't the case now, though. Since he never indulged anyone's curiosity, no one knew much about him. These days, people concocted stories about his past life and the reason he suddenly moved to a small town.

She didn't care about any of that. He seemed like an honest man. He was always polite, even if he never talked much. True that he kept to himself, but there was no law against it, was there?

"You've been mooning over him since the day he moved here. Why don't you ask him out instead of waiting for him?" Cindy teased her.

"Only if I could muster up the courage I absolutely would," Anna sounded wistful.

"Poor you," Cindy's voice was full of mock pity. "I don't like him. Not sure what you see in him. He is so weird."

"Huh? How so?" Anna said. "I'm sure he is just a reserved kind of person and doesn't get frank with people so easily. You can call it weird if you want. I still like him."

"You're such a romantic," her friend and colleague laughed, "you think every brooding man is *Mr. Darcy*. What if he turned out to be *Mr. Wickham*?"

"I don't care either way." Anna believed in the power of love. It didn't matter what kind of person her Kevin was. She was sure that once she could be with him, her love would change him. Although she was certain there wouldn't be any need for that. He was already perfect.

"Miss, can I get a refill?" someone said, getting her attention.

"Well, duty calls," with that, she moved to

appease her customer.

"I'm telling you, this is the last clue we have," one of the men said.

"I hope we find him this time. I'm not sure how long we can afford to chase this man. He is like a ghost," the other one said irritably.

"Your refill," Anna interrupted their chatter.

"Thank you," they said at the same time.

The two men were looking for someone, and she hoped that trouble didn't find their small corner of heaven.

∞∞∞

Kevin wondered if he had overstayed his welcome in this town. People were getting relentless. He feared one of these days someone would uncover his secret and then where would he be? It's not like killing another person was any hardship for him but running away was becoming a nuisance.

He was good at getting rid of the evidence and disposing of bodies. He had lots of practice after all, but he would rather not do it anymore. He was more cautious now as a single mistake could lead him to a lifetime in jail and that must not happen. Life couldn't be *that* cruel to him. He had his share of problems and wanted his life to be smooth sailing from here onwards.

So far, no one seemed to know that he wasn't the owner of the mansion. And he wanted to leave this town before people started getting suspicious or the real owner turned up. He was lucky once in coming across the information that led him to this abandoned mansion in the middle of nowhere. He didn't believe in getting lucky twice. The only problem was that he was no longer sure about his next step. He hadn't decided on a destination yet.

The next day, the whole town was abuzz as the two strangers showed up looking for someone. That couldn't be good news for him. He wondered if someone had found his scent after all. He had tried his best to leave no mark when he fled, but one could never be too sure. He decided not to attract attention to himself and find a way out of there soon.

"Mr. Kevin, your coffee." It was that waitress again. This time, instead of ignoring her, he looked up and gave her his brightest smile.

"Thank you, Miss," he looked at the name tag, "Anna."

It was like Christmas for Anna. He had finally noticed her and even said her name, not to mention he smiled.

"You're welcome." She didn't want this conversation to end.

"You're too nice to me," he sounded genuine. "I wondered if I could have a moment of your time?"

"Now?"

"Not if you're busy, but I could use some company today," he said.

"I'm not busy," she rushed to assure him. "Just give me a minute, and I'll be right with you."

After grabbing a cup of coffee for herself and signaling Cindy to take care of everything, she joined him.

"The truth is that I've been trying to muster up courage and ask you out for quite some time now." He was being coy, as they said desperate times called for desperate measures.

"I'd love to go out with you." She couldn't believe her ears. He was asking her out. Wait, was he asking her out?

"That's a relief," he smiled. So, he was indeed asking her out.

"I wondered when you'd ask," she said, smiling from ear to ear. "How about we grab dinner tonight?"

"You don't waste time," he chuckled, inwardly disgusted at how easily she had agreed to go out with him when she knew nothing about him. *'Is that how the world worked?'* he thought. Anyway, it was all for the best. After inviting her to have dinner at his place, he paid for the coffee and left. The silly starry-eyed waitress would provide him with all the information he needed, and that was all that mattered.

∞∞∞

The doorbell rang, and Kevin invited Anna in. She had made quite an effort to dress up. She was wearing a floral knee-length dress and high-heeled sandals. To be honest, she looked stunning. However, he had plans that couldn't be thwarted, and her beauty had nothing to do with him.

"Do have a seat," he led her into the living room. "Do you want something to drink? Dinner will be ready soon."

"Water is fine." She was nervous and happy at the same time. She hoped that this night would lead to something special in her life. In her mind, Kevin was the one. He was perfect for her, and she would make sure that he loved her as much as she did him.

After the dinner was served, they mostly ate in silence. It was obvious Anna wasn't feeling at home, while Kevin was in his element. Soon, he started talking about the town and the people he had come across. He was no longer the shy and reserved stranger she knew. He steered their conversation towards the two strangers everyone seemed to be talking about.

"I overheard them talking about looking for someone," she said offhandedly, confirming his suspicion. "Maybe they're private investigators or something. I don't know."

"That's interesting, but don't you know almost everyone in town?" he asked.

"Oh, yes, almost but not quite, and then there is you." She gave a nervous giggle.

"But I'm not a stranger now, am I?" he chuckled. "Besides, who could be looking for me? I've no one."

Was that sadness in his voice or something else? For the first time since she had met him, Anna wasn't sure about the person sitting in front of her. She felt as if she was being interrogated. "I'm sorry to hear that. It must be very lonely for you."

"Not at all," this time, he sounded cheerful. "It's very liberating when you've no one to care for. I can be whoever I want and go wherever I feel like going. I'm used to being on my own. It gives me the freedom to live life in my way."

"What do you do?" She wanted to know more about him.

"Well, you know, this and that." He was being vague on purpose.

"So, why did you move to our fair town, if I may ask," she said curiously.

"I inherited this house, so here I am," he

explained.

"You did? I thought you bought it."

"No, I didn't buy it. Some distant relative left it to me. I only recently found out about it. And it was the right time to make a change, so I moved."

"Right, so..." She wasn't sure what to say next. Kevin wanted to know more about what's going on in town. He asked a lot of questions, which she answered. Soon, he had all the information he needed, and he thought it was time to say goodnight.

"Do you mind if I use your washroom?" She said before he could end the night.

"Sure, just go left, follow the hallway, and it's at the end of it."

The house was quite big. There were so many doors along the hallway. She noticed that no photographs were hanging anywhere. She wondered about his family and why he had no photos or anything personal for that matter. He seemed like a loner. Maybe he didn't like putting up photos.

She opened the last door and instead of a washroom, found herself in a walk-in closet or perhaps a storeroom. She must have taken the wrong turn. She was about to go back when her gaze landed on a large photo frame. It looked like a family photo of four people, presumably parents and kids.

As she looked around, she could see that

there was a lot of other stuff thrown haphazardly. There were photos, sports equipment, table games, decoration pieces, and other random things. She wondered why he would keep them here and not display them. Maybe he didn't want the previous owner's photos and things on display, even if they were relatives. Suddenly, the door was jerked open, and Kevin glared at her.

"What are you doing in here?" He asked.

"I must have taken the wrong turn," she said.

However, the answer wasn't enough for him. He was a suspicious person by nature. Above all, he hated nosy people who didn't know how to mind their own business. He wondered what she could've found out among all the junk he had thrown into the room when he first moved here. Maybe she knew the original owners of the house. He couldn't take any risks, especially now that the people were already looking for him. So, he made a decision. Anna would have to go. He couldn't let her live anymore. She should've left when he was done talking to her.

"You shouldn't have come here," he said. "Now, I don't know what you might have discovered." He looked at her menacingly.

"I don't know why you're so upset. I'll leave; I'm sorry. I didn't mean to cause you trouble." She looked scared and wanted to leave as soon as possible.

There was something in his eyes that told her how dangerous the man standing in front of her was. He moved towards her, intending to strangle the woman, when suddenly the doorbell rang. He froze mid-stride and that was enough time for Anna to sidestep and run out the already-opened door. She didn't stop to pick up her things. Instinctively, she knew to get as far away from him as possible. She opened the front door, and the two strangers from earlier were staring at her. Kevin, who was running after her, also stopped in his tracks.

"Mr. Brown, we're here to ask you a few questions about your former neighbor, Mrs. Shelley," one of the men said while holding a badge.

Although it had been a few months, Anna still wondered about Kevin sometimes. Who knew the man she fell in love with would turn out to be a serial killer? Just thinking about how close she came to becoming his next victim gave her shudders. Next time, she would think twice before accepting an invitation from a stranger because that's what he was, and that's what he would ever be.

A stranger who knew no one, and no one ever got to know him.

Together Forever

For unfortunate souls, happily ever after is never something they can choose,

They must fight, all the while hoping for death to lose.

Such is the life of Destiny and Fate—both are doomed to stay apart,

This pain is theirs to bear, and every time they must begin from the start.

They hope and pray to win one day, that's their only sin,

But is winning even an option when they're up against the very world they exist in?

Destiny said nothing. There was nothing for her to say. She felt as if she were dead inside because it hurt so much. Still, she liked to pretend she didn't care. Life had never been easy on her, and she wondered if this was far enough. Maybe it was time to end it all or perhaps start anew. Who knew? She might end up living a better one next time. Although, she was doubtful. She'd never be able to escape this miserable existence.

It was all her fault. Everything. All of it. She had brought it upon herself. She was the one who believed in Fate more than she should've. She was the one who felt all those emotions that weren't hers to feel. She was the one who wanted to change things, and now she would be the one to meet death. Her Fate was cruel, and there would be no turning back time.

"Don't you have anything to say?" Fate said.

"What am I supposed to say? You're right, it's all true. It is my fault," Destiny replied.

"Do you even care?" he asked.

"What do you think?" she countered.

"That's not an answer." He was disappointed.

"No, I don't care," she said at last.

"Liar." He didn't believe her for a second.

"Why ask when you seem to know everything there is to know?" She was annoyed, and rightly so.

"Maybe because I want to hear it from you." He had an answer for everything.

"Or maybe because you don't know as much as you think you do." She smiled one last time.

"Time will tell," he said sadly.

"Indeed, it will," she said, mocking him.

"What now?" he asked as if her answer

mattered.

"Death." Because what else was there anyway?

"Is it really that simple?" he whispered, asking himself more than her.

"Maybe, maybe not, but it's time for me to go."

"Will you ever come back?" he said. Was that regret she heard in his tone?

"If life dictates it to be so. But I'd rather not. I think I have had enough life to last me for eternity." She meant those words.

"I hate to say this, but I agree. It'll be better if you don't come back. I don't want to relive this any more than you do. And I think you might not be able to anyway," he said.

"You must be happy then."

"Ecstatic!" he said while looking anything but.

She smiled then, a sad, soulful smile that would haunt him forever. She was gone, hopefully, never to return. He was free. He hated this freedom, but he loved it, too. The past was cruel to them both, the present not much better, but the future might be theirs to hold. He hoped she was at peace. She deserved that much after all she had endured, a whole lifetime of torment. They were both helpless against life and death. They hadn't chosen this existence. It was given to them, and there was no escaping it. Rules weren't meant to be broken. Not here. Not anywhere.

∞∞∞

Fate saw the moment hope left her eyes. He saw exactly when her heart froze, but he couldn't stop himself. It was for her good. She needed a dose of reality to bring back the balance. The balance was tripped because of their foolishness.

They had been selfish and careless in their pursuit of happiness and love. Foolish! Love wasn't for them. Happiness wasn't for them. He knew better. Balance must be maintained, or the multiverse would have to pay dearly. It could all be destroyed in one single moment of carelessness on their part.

He couldn't let that happen. It was for the greater good, as they said. Today, he'd let his love die once again and save everyone else. Perhaps someday, under better circumstances, she would return to stay. For now, this was it. The end that would bring new beginnings.

"At least you didn't let me die in vain this time," Destiny said.

"Never! Never that." He was sadder than he had ever been before.

"You did well." She was smiling and looking at him with approval.

"I hope so."

"We shall meet again, you know. But it won't be love."

"I know. Our love was doomed from the start. But let's meet again anyway." He agreed.

"I shall hate you forever," she said softly. She didn't want to give him false hope.

"I'd expect nothing less," he said, his voice full of regret.

"You never believed in us," she complained, pouting.

"You're wrong, I believed, maybe a little too much." He had hoped for the best, too.

"Then why did you give up?" she asked.

"I didn't. This isn't giving up," he tried to explain.

"What else is it?"

"Some sacrifices must be made."

"Ah! Always the martyr," she said laughingly.

"Always."

"I hope you can endure what comes next." She warned.

"Me too. I am ready."

"But I'm not. Maybe I never will be, but I must go now, for death awaits."

He saw her take her last breath, and then she was no more. Life demanded it to be so, so it must be. They weren't meant to be together. One had to perish, and he made sure it wasn't him. Never him. He felt different, though. This time, it was more painful than before. He hoped she would forgive him someday, but he knew that might not happen. She was fierce that way, his Destiny. She could never let go of her anger. Oh, and how angry she must have been? He had betrayed her again. He wished it was the last time, but some wishes weren't meant to come true.

They said the third time's a charm. Perhaps this time, no one would have to die. This time, love might withstand it all. But it was too much to ask for.

She remembered, and she hated it. That had never happened before. She had never hated him. He wondered what she had in mind for him. He knew it would be nothing good.

"You must have known this was coming," she said. Her voice was laced with hatred.

"Yes, I expected this much. You're still as beautiful as ever." He was resigned to his fate.

"Flattery won't help you. Not this time. This time, I remember it all from the very beginning."

"That's a twist I wasn't anticipating."

"Ha! You must be so surprised then." She was

proud of herself.

"I am." He was defeated.

"It matters not. I'm leaving. I shall never come back." This time, she wasn't going to die for him.

"You can't do that. You can't just leave like that. Balance must be kept. This is our duty. Besides, there is nowhere to go," he said, a little scared of what might happen.

"As if I'd care about duties? And you don't know everything."

"You must understand. You're pragmatic. You must see the wisdom in what I did." What was he asking her anyway? The ball was in her court now. She must decide.

"You broke my heart, and you killed me. Not once, but many times. Every time," she said furiously.

"It was the right thing to do. It's something that's meant to happen." After all, it wasn't like he wanted it to happen, for her to die.

"Not this time. This time is different. I know a secret even you don't know."

"There are no secrets here," he said, giving her an annoyed look.

"Oh, yes, but there is one." She looked like the cat that got the cream.

"No!" He was afraid. Was she going to kill him now? He wondered what death would feel like and how long until he was reborn.

But she didn't kill him. That was never her intention. Even in her hatred, she loved him. She took him with her, though. They both left their plane of existence together. It wasn't that she didn't understand the balance. It was only that she was tired of losing to him, losing him. She was tired of life winning every single time.

It had to end, and she made it happen. Multiverse was no more. After all, this time, she knew the truth. She had changed her ways, and he had to follow. She wasn't going to leave him behind to perish. No, they needed to find happiness together, and so they did, in a way.

From here onwards, life must not interfere with their existence. Now, they would be the ones controlling it. They had come to a place where they could be together without tripping the balance. This world belonged to them both equally. Here, they were the same. Life bowed down to them, and death didn't stand a chance either. All the while, hope ruled supreme.

Fate and Destiny, together, forever.

Chasing a Ghost

He came to me in a dream. A dream that took my breath away and left me gasping. I hadn't been able to get him out of my mind. Sometimes consciously and sometimes unconsciously, my eyes searched for him in the crowds. Everywhere I went, his ghost followed me. Every time I looked at a stranger, for a second I would wonder, "Is it him?" I knew it sounded absurd. It was a dream, and dreams weren't real. I didn't even know why this man had taken hold of my heart. I only knew I had to find him, or I would go insane.

Then I did find him, but in the process, I ruined everything good in my life.

∞ ∞ ∞

"Mama," not-so-little Savera still needed her mother, "please, I can't do it on my own."

"You must try, sweetheart," her mother replied. Savera was growing up so fast, but the girl depended on her mother for all the little and big things.

"Hold the needle like this," she showed her daughter, "there's nothing to it." All she wanted for her daughter was to learn the things all girls should know. Her daughter was her life. She loved that amazingly sweet girl.

"Why must I sew this? Can't you do it for me?" Savera was pouting. She hated that her mother wouldn't do chores for her anymore. It all started last month. Before that, she never had to do anything herself because her mother took care of everything. Not anymore, though. These days, her mother would make her do all kinds of things around the house. "Baba, can't you ask Mama to do it for me?" She looked at her father as a last resort. Her father was always on her side. Today, even he wasn't in the mood to indulge her.

"Listen to your mother, Severa," he said distractedly, "you aren't a child anymore."

And so, she was learning the hard way. In her mind, it wasn't fair. Why must she work around the house when she has schoolwork? What did her mother do all day long? She was the one who stayed at home. It was her job to take care of everything for them. Her father worked hard. He often got home tired to the bone. She studied hard. She wanted to be a doctor, unlike her mother, who was a housewife. What did her mother do all day?

"It's for your good, dear," her mother said. "You must learn cooking, sewing, laundry, and dishes. I won't be with you forever. It's time for you to learn how to run a house."

"But I don't want to learn all that." She still couldn't understand what the fuss was about. "I'm going to become a doctor. I'll have a job to worry about. I can hire people to do house chores for me."

Her mother smiled at that. The little girl had big ambitions. "That doesn't matter. If you don't want to do it, that's okay too. But you need to know how to, at least."

"Oh, okay," she smiled at last, "did I do it right?" She showed her work to her mother, who kissed her forehead and told her it was perfect.

It wasn't, though. Nothing in their lives was perfect. Soon, Savera would find out what had changed. For now, she believed her mother's reasoning for teaching her things she didn't even need to learn.

∞∞∞

"Why do you do that?" Her husband asked her later that night.

"Do what?" She knew what he meant but didn't want to admit it.

"You know what I'm talking about. Savera is a child. She doesn't need to work around the house. I don't work this hard to see my daughter worry about silly things like dishes or laundry. If you don't want to do it, then hire a maid. Have I ever asked you not to?"

"You're like her, or rather she's like you." She looked at her husband lovingly and said, "You two never see what's right in front of you."

"What's that supposed to mean?"

"You know, being a housewife was my choice. I know we can hire help, but I don't want to. And I teach her these things because I don't want her to depend on others for little things in life."

Her husband looked at her like she was an enigma, a puzzle he couldn't solve.

"I won't always be here," she said in a voice laced with sadness and something more. Was that regret he heard in his wife's voice?

"Why would you say something like that?" He looked at her, seeing her at last and realizing something he had been ignoring for quite some time now. "You're leaving me?" He said it as a question, but in his heart, he already knew the answer. His wife of eight years was no longer in love with him. Oh, she loved him still, there was no doubt, but she wasn't in love, and there was nothing he could do about it.

She said nothing and looked at him helplessly. "I don't know how to explain this."

"At least tell me the reason. Did I do something wrong? Are you not happy? What about Savera?" Those were only a few of the questions he wanted to ask her. This woman amazing and kind woman he fell in love with at first sight had been his entire life. She was his universe. She was the light of his dark nights. He loved her with all his heart, and he couldn't believe she was thinking of leaving him—leaving them. How could she? What had he missed?

"It's not you, it's not this life, it's me... there is someone..."

He couldn't hear anymore. He got out of the bed and left the room. There was no way he could lie there and listen to his wife telling him she loved someone else.

∞ ∞ ∞

"She's your mother, sweetheart," he said to Savera. "She loves you. Even though what she did to me was wrong, it had nothing to do with you."

"I don't know, Baba," Savera said. "How can you be so forgiving? She ruined our lives. I don't want to see her. I don't even want to hear her name."

"But she wants to see you. She misses you."

"Boo hoo, if she loved me so much, she should've stayed with you, with us. She left. We were here. Do you know how many nights I have stayed awake waiting for her to show up? But she didn't." There was no getting through to her. She had hated her mother for many years now. A mother who left her to chase after a dream... A dream that wasn't to be. Who did that? "She is dead to me."

"Savera!" He chastised his daughter. He knew his ex-wife was standing behind the door, waiting for their daughter to see her and hug her after all these years. But their daughter wasn't ready to let a runaway mother back into her life or her heart. "See her once. Let her explain it."

"No." With that, Savera ran up to her room.

Disheartened by his daughter's behavior, he had no option but to let his ex-wife know that today wasn't the day.

"I heard, and it's okay. She needs time. Besides, it's my fault." There wasn't anything she could do about it anyway.

"I'm sorry. I'll try talking to her again. She'll come around, I'm sure."

"Thank you."

$$\infty \infty \infty$$

She didn't stay after that. There was no reason to. Savera was right. She had ruined her family while chasing after a dream. But she couldn't help it. She saw him in her dream and fell in love with him, irrevocably in love.

She knew she was being silly. She knew he wasn't real. Yet, she couldn't help searching for him.

She had to try and find him. That man had her heart, and she couldn't, in good conscience, stay with her husband after that. It was selfish and cruel, and she did break three hearts when she decided to go after a shadow.

That wasn't everything, though. She had found him, the man from her dream. She met him one day while shopping. He was a salesman at a dress shop. He was exactly how she saw him in her dreams, handsome and amazing. But no matter how much she tried, she couldn't make him fall in love with her.

He had a family of his own. And he refused to leave them for a crazy woman who fell in love with him because she thought she saw him in a dream. He must have thought her insane. At least he didn't report her as a stalker or had her committed. That was something. After spending years chasing after someone who didn't want her, she decided to give up. That was when she thought of her daughter. Now, there she was, trying to mend something she had broken herself. Did she even deserve forgiveness? She wasn't so sure.

I felt sorry for her. She is only the shell of a woman I fell in love with all those years ago. And if I were honest with myself, I would admit I still loved her. The sadness in her eyes all but broke my heart. What happened to her? Why would she follow someone from a dream, like a crazy person? I knew she was helpless because of her intense feelings for someone she hadn't met. But there wasn't anything I could do to make her stay.

In all this, the one who suffered the most was her. That woman was not the same. She was no longer the person she used to be. She was back, but could she make up for the past? Perhaps Savera had a point, and there was no second chance for someone as impulsive as her. Or maybe there was still hope for a new beginning.

If you chase after a ghost, you're bound to end up broken.

A Dream That Never Was

We all have stories that we don't wish to tell others. It's not always easy to hide them because some skeletons refuse to be safely tucked away in the closet. That's how this terrible, horrible story began, with a secret that should've remained a secret but didn't.

"Susan, sweetheart, where are you?" I called out to my wife as soon as I crossed the threshold of our front door. It was an important day, and I wanted everything to be perfect.

"Give me five minutes, and I'll be down," she shouted back from our room.

She wasn't ready. I hated it when she took so much time to get ready. But she was obsessed with looking perfect, and I usually tried to be patient, letting her take her time.

"I'm ready." She was all smiles today.

I looked up then, she was coming down the stairs. I must admit, she took my breath away. Although we had been married for ten years, I still felt like a newlywed who kept falling in love with his wife every time he saw her. She was the most beautiful woman on this planet.

"You look stunning, darling," I told her, taking her in my arms and kissing her in a way she wouldn't forget any time soon.

"Thank you. You look good yourself," she replied, giving me her best smile.

I loved her smile. Her smile was the first thing I had noticed about her. It was warm and welcoming. Before I fell in love with her, I fell in love with her smile.

"I love it when you smile like that," I told her. I could never let any opportunity to tell her that pass me by. After all, it was my life's purpose to put a smile on her pretty face and keep it there.

"I'm the luckiest woman in the world." She sounded content.

"And that, my love, makes me the happiest man in the world," I said.

Sometimes, it all felt like a dream. She was so out of my league. I still remember how everyone told me she would never fall for me, but somehow, she did. I didn't know why or how, but that gorgeous, accomplished, and independent woman fell in love with me. With years, our love had only grown stronger. If it was a dream, then I never wanted to wake up.

"Let's go, we shouldn't be late," she reminded me.

As we left our house, I wondered how much better our lives were about to get. Today was our tenth wedding anniversary. In itself, it was a happy day, but what made it perfect was the fact that we were about to become parents. We had finalized everything, and now we had to go pick up our adopted daughter. Our family would be complete now.

Life was perfect ... until it wasn't.

What was the best day of my life soon turned into a nightmare. James wasn't supposed to find out the truth. I had hidden it well. No one even knew my real name. To them, I was Susan Johnson, James' wife, a doctor who cared for her patients more than anything else. I was successful and rich. I was beautiful and kind. I was a woman of every man's dream. And my James was perfect for me. He loved me. He adored me. To him, I was everything.

Some might think me lucky, but luck had nothing to do with it. I sold my soul to the devil to get everything I had in my life. It wasn't a decision I made lightly, and I knew one day, I would have to pay dearly. Only, I didn't know that day would come so soon or in such a devastating way.

"Say hello to your parents, dear. These nice people are here to take you home." The social worker coaxed the child, who refused to budge from her seat. She was afraid and feeling unsure of herself.

"That's right, love, we're here to take you home. Do you want to go with us?"

I tried my best mommy voice, or at least what I thought it was. It worked because the child gave me a small smile. That was progress. I was already in love with our daughter.

"It'll be perfect. Don't you worry about anything," James said.

I could understand his happiness because I was feeling it, too. Being a parent is all I wanted in life.

Soon, we had all her things and were on our way home. A home that was about to become so much warmer and more welcoming. James would be a great father, that much I knew. I hoped I would turn out to be a great mother, too. Not that I had any idea what a great mother should be like. I would figure it out. I was determined to make this little family work and to keep my dream intact.

Unfortunately, it wasn't to be.

It happened all at once. There was nothing Susan or I could have done. The car came out of nowhere and crushed ours. Just like that, our daughter died before we even reached home. There was no going home for any of us. Our dream died with her.

When I thought about it, I realized how strange it was. Our paradise was no more. After ten years of pure bliss, it was the darkness that surrounded us. Susan and I were both utterly lost. We could have come out of our grief, though. With time, we could have found our happiness again, but along with our daughter, our love died too. I couldn't forgive Susan for betraying me the way she did. Only if she had told me the truth. Only if I knew everything before we decided to adopt.

∞∞∞

"How long are you going to hate me?" she said as if she were the victim.

"Forever, you betrayed me. Nothing was real. I can't forgive you. I hate that you lied to me for so long." Nothing she could say was going to unfreeze my broken heart.

"I meant well. You know I did. I love you. I always have." She tried again.

"Love? Do you even know what love is?" I asked bitterly.

"James, please, don't be so stubborn. It has been two years now." She looked at me helplessly as if she could ever be helpless.

"To me, it feels like yesterday. I cannot forget it." I had tried, after all.

"Will you ever?"

"I don't think so." This time, I didn't look into her eyes. I feared I was lying to us both. I couldn't help it. My brain was telling me to forgive her, to move on, but my heart was in pieces, and I wasn't ready to let go of the past.

"We were happy once," she reminded me of the time I was trying to forget.

"Yes, but now I know that was an illusion." Who were we kidding?

"What does it matter? We were happy. Isn't that enough?" She was getting desperate.

"Go find your happiness somewhere else, with someone else. I'm done with you. Why do you keep coming here?" I hated that she wouldn't leave me alone. Even after two years, she showed up at my home and asked for forgiveness that I wasn't willing to give.

"Okay, I'll go for now. But I'll come back. Maybe you'll change your mind then," with that she left.

She was wrong. I would never change my mind. I was going to leave. My flight was already booked. I wasn't going to tell anyone. I was simply going to move to some third-world country whose name

I couldn't pronounce, and I wasn't coming back. There was nothing left for me here. My life was nothing more than a dream, but I was awake now. Unfortunately, I couldn't go back to sleep, no matter how hard I tried.

You might be wondering what was the secret that destroyed us. It was nothing. That's what it was. I was never in love with Susan. We were never happy. She wasn't even the woman I thought she was. It was all a lie. Everything was a lie.

She had created this illusion, and I had accepted it without question. I saw what she showed me. I felt what she told me to feel. I was living in a haze. For ten years, nothing was real until that accident. When our daughter died, Susan lost her powers. Her true face was revealed to me then. And with that, this feeling crept up inside me, this gnawing feeling of being betrayed by the person I thought I loved.

It was all gone. In a single moment, our life crumbled like a house of cards. Maybe I overreacted. After all, even if happiness was an illusion, it was beautiful. But I couldn't get it out of my head. I couldn't forgive her for tricking me and betraying my trust.

Who knew my James could hold a mean grudge? I hoped and waited, but he never forgave me. He was lost to me, and I didn't know what to do. True, I lied and betrayed him, but in the end, I fell in love with him. Not that he would ever believe me now. I'd have to live with this hole in my life.

Do you know what the worst thing was? He would die and be with our daughter someday. I couldn't even do that. I was going to spend eternity with my regrets.

I sold my soul, and I became an immortal. That was centuries ago. I was not beautiful. I was rich, though, beyond your imagination. I had spent much time on this planet alone. Then, I got tired of being alone and decided to create my paradise.

I chose James because he was the kindest soul I knew. I made him believe that he loved me and that he was happy with me. I created an illusion of a perfect life and lived it with him. But something was still missing, and that's when I decided to become a parent. Humans say nothing in life is more beautiful than that. Immortals couldn't give birth, so we decided to adopt. I didn't know, though. Immortals weren't allowed to have children for a reason. It was an unspoken rule of the universe, and I dared break it.

She was killed and my illusion was broken.

Rules weren't meant to be broken. The universe demanded a balance to be kept no matter what. And this was my punishment, an eternity without James and our daughter.

∞∞∞

Life plays jokes on us sometimes. Things we want to see are shown to us, and when we accept them as truths, suddenly, we find out that they are nothing but lies.

We hate what we don't understand. We hate what we can't control. We all have our prejudices. The universe is messed up in certain ways. Not that we can do anything about it, but that doesn't stop us from trying either.

I once knew an immortal. I miss her sometimes. I wonder where she is now. I hope she is happy somewhere, without me. I wish I had forgiven her, but I didn't want to live in an illusion. I wanted reality. As painful as it is, I love it, this life, it's mine. This pain, too, makes me human, and I love being human.

We all have prejudices, even if we like to pretend otherwise. Yes, I was prejudiced against non-humans. But that was a long time ago. I know better now. These days I try not to be so judgmental and be more forgiving. After all, I was living a dream that many would kill to live.

Yet, some dreams are not to be.

All That We Know

Almost all girls dream about their happily ever after. It's something that everyone knows girls do. Sara was no different. Since the day she met Zain, she had been dreaming of a future with him, a future full of hope and love. Zain, however, didn't even know she existed. He was aloof and self-absorbed. For him, the only person worth loving was himself. Poor Sara, she was in a world of trouble. But that would turn out to be the least of her worries. Life could be so tricky at times. Wouldn't you agree?

∞∞∞

"I had a dream once where I was happy and loved," I tell Hania. "I never thought I'd end up in a relationship that would suck all my energy, leaving me broken and battered."

"At least you are free now. There's still life ahead of you. You can start over, and maybe this time you will find your happily ever after," Hania says.

She is an optimist, which I admire. The only

problem is that I no longer believe in love or happy endings. I'm sad and need someplace secluded to live the rest of my life in peace. I have suffered enough and am not ready to let people in. People only brought trouble. They are good for nothing, and I plan to stay away from them, as far away as possible.

I don't know how it is for others, but my brain catalogs things as unimportant and then buries them underneath all the things it perceives to be important. That's why I don't always remember everything. I have limited long-term memory.

I rarely remember things that I won't use in life anyway. Also, the funny thing is that the few things I remember don't make much sense. They shape my present. I know their importance, but they don't let me connect with people.

Sometimes, I wonder if these memories are real or just manifestations of my demons. I don't know much, which is annoying when you think about it. Most days, my brain is mush and I hate it. I have learned to live with it, though. I'm one of those people who accept their reality quickly rather than keep trying to change it, which is almost always futile.

This is my life, and it's not perfect by any means, but I'm happy. As happy as anyone on this planet can be. I live alone. I have my books to keep me company. Don't get me wrong, I have a family and friends I'm close to. They visit me often, and sometimes I visit them. I cherish solitude that's all.

I met Sara at one of my family dinners. She is my sister's best friend. Lately, she has been invited to every family gathering I have been to. I wonder what my sister is up to. Nothing good if I know her well, which I think I do.

"Hi," Sara says, "it's good to see you again."

"Is it?" I reply, "I thought you hated me."

"What? Why would you think that?" She looks taken aback.

"Well, probably because of your frown? Every time we talk, you've got this annoyed look on your face," I say matter-of-factly.

"I do?" She asks in a shocked tone.

It's as if that comes as a surprise to her. Doesn't she know that she has never smiled at me? Not even once, in all these times, we have known each other. Sometimes, I wonder what her story is, then I decide it's none of my damned business.

"I'm sorry. I never noticed it," she blushed with embarrassment. "It's not that I dislike you or talking to you. I'm just not comfortable around men in general."

"Good to know," I say. "I was beginning to think you hated me."

"What are you two talking about?" Hania says, entering the kitchen just then.

"Oh, nothing important," Sara says hastily. "Let's go out. I want to enjoy the bonfire."

Taking my sister's hand, Sara drags her out. Just before leaving, Hania gives me a weird look. I know what she is trying to do, and I do like Sara, but she is too serious and stuffy. And also, I'm not interested in having a relationship at the moment. Maybe never. I need to sort out my life first. There are secrets in my past that even I don't know about.

I love them both, my best friend and brother, but they are such idiots. I know how much they love each other. I don't understand why they can't see what's right in front of them.

People can be so silly. I guess this is how life is. We make up lies in our heads and they don't let us see the truth. Take Sara, for example. She says she doesn't believe in love anymore. I don't believe it for a second. She is hurt that much is obvious, but she is healing too, and I know for a fact that she loves my brother.

My brother, on the other hand, thinks he doesn't need anyone except his books. Ridiculous! What am I going to do with these two idiots?

Me? Well, I'm the kind of person who lives in the moment. I'm not someone who makes up lies in her head instead I let the world show me everything it wants me to see. I don't know what I want from life, but I know I want to be happy. And I want everyone I love to be happy, too.

The only two things that are important to me are happiness and love. I also think that they go hand in hand. That's why I'm bent upon making my brother see sense. Then, he can convince Sara to give up on the notion of a loveless life. Why would anyone want that?

My heart breaks to see my friend so sad. She needs someone in her life, and I will make sure that she finds him. They are perfect for each other, and they must realize it before it is too late.

"Hania, I need your help," one of my roommates shouts from the other room. They always want something from me. I'm thinking of moving out of this dump soon. Sharing a place with three self-absorbed divas is no fun, I tell you.

The day Zain left me in the hospital, broken and battered from the tragedy that had befallen us, my life took a turn I never imagined it would.

This is life, though. Things happen unexpectedly, and we adapt accordingly. That day, I not only lost our unborn child but also my husband, the only man I have ever truly loved.

Zain was a strange person. I always knew that. He was different, and that's what attracted me to him. Soon, I realized that different doesn't always mean good. He was abusive, not physically but emotionally. With him, I was never happy, but without him, I'm still unhappy.

I was depressed for a long time after that. Finally, I am fine. At least, I think that I am. I have gathered all the broken pieces of my heart and put them together, all on my own. I'm in a good place and don't want to change anything that might disturb my newfound peace.

Hania, however, seems to think I need a man in my life to make it complete. I would never understand why people think that way. Is it hard to believe that I can be happy without a man?

"I'm your friend," she says, "And I want what's best for you."

"And you think your brother is what's best for me?" I'm annoyed with her.

"Look, he likes you. I know he does," she adds quickly before I can say anything, "I also happen to know that you like him. Why don't you two go on a date? If it isn't meant to be, then that's fine. I'll stop pestering you, but at least give it a try. I know you are both perfect for each other."

"Why do you think I need to date?"

"Have you ever wondered maybe it's not you but him I think that about?"

"Huh?" I certainly hadn't thought of it that way.

"I know you're an independent woman. I understand your fears and your lack of interest in having a relationship. I also know you don't need anyone but yourself to be happy. You're forgetting that I was there, with you, when your idiot husband left you. I have seen your strength, and that's exactly why I think you're perfect for my brother."

"What do you mean? What's wrong with your brother?"

"Nothing is wrong with him. I worry about his lack of dating life. Do you know he has never dated anyone at all?" She sighs.

"Never?" Wow, that's strange.

"Never!"

That is indeed an interesting and disturbing fact. He looks like a model, he is rich, and I'm sure many girls would love to go out with him, so why has he never dated? I don't think even Hania knows, or she would tell me. We have no secrets, the two of us.

"So, what do you say?" She prompts me when I'm quiet for a while.

"Okay then, but one date."

"Yes!"

"Don't get too excited. It's just one date."

I must admit I'm curious about him now. I want to know his story. I want to be the person who will heal his wounds if there are any. I will teach him how to make his life worth living even without anyone to share it with. Suddenly, I have a new purpose in life that might not be all bad.

$$\infty \infty \infty$$

My sister is such a pest. I'm not even sure how she managed it, but she finally convinced us to go on a date. And here we are. Sara is the most beautiful woman I have ever met, and I like her. It's not about her as such. I don't like dating.

"I hear you've never dated before," she says.

I'm going to kill my sister for telling her that little bit of personal information. "I don't usually find time for that kind of thing."

"That's just an excuse, don't you think?" She smiles.

"I don't know, there's no other reason." I shrug.

"You do like women, though. I mean, you aren't gay, right? Not that there's anything wrong with it, but then this date would be pointless." She is flustered, which I find cute.

"Don't worry, it's nothing like that," I laughed, "as I said, there's no specific reason. I just never thought about it."

"What do you do when you get bored?" she asks.

"I don't get bored. I read." I pointed out with a smile. Just thinking about reading can improve my mood.

"Ah! You're the bookish type then," she says as if that explains everything.

"So?" I ask a bit defensively.

"Oh, nothing," she continues, "I just love nerdy men."

"What?" I chuckle, "Are you saying that you love me?"

"Huh? No! That's not what I meant," she adds hastily, "You know it's not."

"Relax, I'm kidding."

"So, do you think you will date me?"

"Do you want me to?" I ask.

"I think I do," she says at last.

"Then I will." And that's how our love story begins.

We enjoy each other's company, and I'm beginning to like her even more. I don't think she is stuffy. Now that I'm getting to know her, I think she is cautious, and that's good. I hope this thing works out for both of us. I would hate to cause my sister any pain. I know how close the two women are. Hurting Sara means hurting Hania, and that's the last thing I'd ever want to do. It didn't even occur to me that she might end up hurting me.

∞ ∞ ∞

Shan turned out to be one of the good guys. He is considerate, and he makes me laugh. Slowly, he is breaking the ice around my heart. I'm beginning to fall in love with him. I thought I'd never love anyone again, yet he is easy to love. There is something about him that puts my mind at ease.

When I'm with him, I don't fear as much as I thought I would. I want to tell him everything and for him to return the favor. He doesn't, though. I can feel his reluctance to share most private parts of his life. Or maybe he isn't the sharing kind of person.

"Are you alright?" I ask Shan.

"I'm fine," he smiles, "What do you want to watch?"

"Pride and Prejudice."

"No, please, not again," he groans. "How many times have we watched that movie? I think this time I should choose."

"I was kidding," I say teasingly. "I just got this new movie, so let's watch that today."

"That's exciting."

I open my eyes and see Shan looking at me oddly.

"What?" I ask, not realizing I had fallen asleep while watching the movie.

"You fell asleep," he says as if that is all the

answer I need. But it doesn't explain why he looks at me as if I'm a puzzle to solve.

"Sorry about that," I say, still disoriented.

"You were talking in your sleep," he whispers.

"I was?" I hope I didn't say something too embarrassing.

"I just," he looks for words. "Hmm, I didn't know about your past."

"Hania didn't tell you?" I assumed she must have.

"No. I'm sorry that you went through something so painful." He looks at me with sympathy.

I'm used to such looks. They have never bothered me. "It was a long time ago." I give him a warm smile.

It's true I no longer feel the pain that used to come with these memories. Now, I'm at peace with my life.

"You're such a powerful woman. I love that about you."

"Are you saying you love me?" This time, I tease him.

"Yeah, I think I am," he says, surprising us both and rendering me speechless.

"It's okay, and I know you aren't there yet. I'm a patient man. I will wait for you," he says when I don't respond to his comment.

∞ ∞ ∞

I hope I did the right thing. I've never seen my brother so happy. Shan is in love, and it shows. I'm sure Sara loves him too, even if she hasn't realized it yet. She will soon because my friend is stubborn, but she isn't stupid.

"Do you know why Shan has never dated before?" Sara asks me once again.

"No, it never came up. We assumed that he didn't want to. It's not like there is any tragic story there," I say.

"Are you sure?" She is doubtful.

"Yep, why?" I wonder if she knows something I don't.

"No reason, it just bothers me. He is so loving and kind. I find it hard to believe that he has never dated or fallen in love before now."

"Believe it. I wouldn't lie to you." I smile at my friend, giving her a half hug.

"I trust you," she says, hugging me back.

"Thankfully, or I didn't know what I might have done to make you believe."

It is late at night. I'm with Shan, and we are discussing where our relationship is headed. About some things, he is so open and straightforward. But about others, he can be so tight-lipped.

"Are you sure you want me to move in?" I ask again.

"Absolutely," he says, "I told you I love you."

"And you're okay that I haven't said those words back?" I'm almost scared to hear his answer.

"I know you love me, even if you're not ready to say it out loud. I have told you I can wait." He reassures me.

I'm not sure how he is so confident. Perhaps he knows me better than I know myself. I don't say anything after that. He is right. I think I love him. Why can't I say those dreaded words to him is beyond me. What is wrong with me? Here I am with a kind man, who loves me and is willing to be patient, but I still can't tell him I love him, too.

"Hey, you're thinking too much. It's okay, don't be hard on yourself. I know why you find it difficult to say those words. You've said them before, and it didn't go well for you." Not surprisingly, that makes perfect sense.

"You're right. I'm sure that's the reason." I hope that's all there is to it.

"Don't worry. I'll never leave you no matter what," he says, and I believe him.

I know he also believes it, which is why I trust

him. Maybe this is what I have been waiting for. Shan is the man I need. Life has brought him to me. The time is right, and everything is perfect. I think life will be beautiful from now on.

"I love you, too," I tell him in a whisper.

"You just made me the happiest man in the world. Marry me," he says.

"What?" I'm shocked, which you may have guessed, "You're serious?"

"Please, say yes."

"Yes," I say at last. Hoping against hope, I won't regret my words later.

I don't know where I got the courage to say yes to his out-of-the-blue proposal. I know I want to marry him and be with him forever. I want a family with him, and I don't care what secret about his life he is hiding, as long as it's in the past, which I think it is.

∞∞∞

"We are engaged," Shan announces in front of his family.

They are all overjoyed, especially Hania. She is happy for us. Life can't get any better than this. I have known many people and seen many faces. Among all of them, his is the face I want to keep seeing for the rest of my life.

"I was right to push you two to date," Hania says, looking smug.

"You were," Shan replies and smiles, "little sister."

"Who knew you were such a romantic, big brother," she teases him.

"Honestly, even I didn't know," he admits.

"I'm happy I found you. I love this romantic side of you," I say.

"I love you too, baby," he replies.

"Awe, look at these two lovebirds. I hope your entire life is as perfect as this moment," his mother says, tearing up.

At this moment, we are all happy. But, you see, this is the thing about happiness: it rarely lasts. I wonder how long mine will last this time around. Forever might just be too much to hope for.

We got married last month. And after marriage, I have discovered the dreaded secret my husband has been hiding from everyone for so long. Most of his memories aren't real. He thinks they are, but they are not.

It has only been a month, and his entire recollection of our wedding day is fiction. He doesn't remember a single thing that happened that day.

What he remembers never happened. I don't know how to deal with this. Sometimes, it gets too much for me to handle.

I tell him how things unfolded, but he keeps insisting on his version of the events. Not that there is anything wrong with his version, except it's not true. I don't know what's the extent of his problem. I wonder if someday he will wake up and forget that he loves me. Do you think that can happen?

Fear has taken root in my heart. I don't smile anymore. I don't laugh. I love Shan so much and I fear he will leave me just like Zain did. Right now, he loves me, but for how long is anyone's guess?

"I don't know what to say, Sara," Hania is shocked at my revelation. "I mean, we have always noticed how he gets facts wrong. All our childhood stories are different when he tells them. We all just assumed his memory was weak. Lots of people forget their childhood memories. We've never noticed him do that about his recent memories."

"But how often do you see him? How much do you know about his life right now?" I ask, desperation seeping into my voice.

"We only see each other at family gatherings. You know that. It has been years since we lived in the same house." She is thoughtful now, but I don't think she has any answers for me.

"Oh, Hania, I am so scared," I say.

"Don't be. I'm sure it's nothing," Hania says,

trying to calm me down.

She is wrong, though. It isn't nothing. It's the most important thing. I'm afraid it will cause trouble for us down the road.

∞∞∞∞

Something is different about my wife. She looks at me weirdly. She has never looked at me like that before. I'm not sure what it is, but I hope she gets over it.

Like last night when she argued with me about the color of her dress. I remember she wore black to the party. But for some reason, she has been insisting that she wore red.

Absurd, even the pictures show her black dress. She is losing her mind, I think. I have shown her the photos and still, she keeps insisting, "Look, it's red." I wonder if I've married a mad woman. I hope not.

I love her so much. And I can't lose her to madness. It doesn't matter. I will love her even if she is mad. I will always love her. She is my one true love, my soulmate.

"What are you thinking about, honey," Sara says.

"Nothing important. I'm wondering what my wife is up to these days," I say.

"Just the usual, you know."

She doesn't smile, which I find troubling. She seems down. I try to bring up a topic I know she will love to talk about. "So, you joined your classes again?" I ask in the hope of seeing her passion. She is passionate about her education.

"What classes?" she asks, confused and annoyed.

"You know, the usual." Did I say something wrong again?

"Ah, yeah, I did." She doesn't elaborate. The passion is missing, and so is her smile.

Why does she look so sad? Have I done something wrong? How will I live with a woman so prone to mood swings? I hope our love endures it all.

∞∞∞

It breaks my heart when I see them. Shan has gotten worse. These days, he can hardly remember anything at all. Sara is struggling with his problem. She is human, too. I don't know how long she will be able to tolerate him.

He thinks she is going mad. He told me that he wants her to get treatment, but she won't. I told him that she was fine and he was the one with fake memories. He blew a casket, and we fought for the first time in our adult lives. The saddest part is that he doesn't even remember it anymore.

My brother and his wife, my best friend, are not happy these days. My brother doesn't know this, and my friend can't forget it. The two of them are doomed to live in misery.

So, this is life. Sara loves him so much that she refuses to leave him. Shan loves her so much that he refuses to remember anything bad about their marriage. His memories are perfect. In his mind, she gets upset over nothing. Maybe, in the end, they will manage to get along. Or they might destroy each other. For now, all we can do is pray and hope for the best.

"I did the right thing to introduce them, though, didn't I?" I ask.

Unfortunately, my therapist has no answer for me.

Death, I Don't Fear

Life is always uncertain, and we all die someday. I, however, know the exact time of my impending death. I don't know how, I don't know where, but I know that on December 22, 2019, I will die. I've always known that. You might think that it must have prepared me for death, but no such luck. All my life, I have just ignored this knowledge. Now, I only have one year left to live. And I have come to realize that there is so much I still need to do. One year would never be enough. Sometimes I wonder if I'm crazy and this is just paranoia. But in my heart, I know this to be true. Death is looking for me and is very close to finding me.

"Mahir, why are you up here?" Mahreen asked, peeking through the door.

Her voice startled me as I had been deep in thought. "Nothing. I was looking for things to donate. There is so much junk here. I never bothered with it before, but now I feel it's time to get rid of everything I no longer need," I said.

"That's a good idea," she said, looking around and scrunching her nose at what she perceived as garbage and clutter.

Mahreen was my best friend. She had minor OCD, and sometimes she really couldn't tolerate being around me. I was a scattered brain, as everyone told me. Nothing in my home or my life was in order. I had never noticed this before, but now I could see why my parents always told me to get it together. I had been living my life one day at a time, never worried about the future. I guess it's because deep down, something in me always knew I wouldn't live for long, so why bother?

"The important question is, how come you're here? Did you come to see me?" I asked.

Where I was the one to live in the moment, she was my exact opposite. Usually, every word out of her mouth was preplanned. She always thought before she talked. She contemplated twice before she took a step. I had never known her to show up without planning it first.

"Duh!" She exclaimed. "Why else would I be at your home and in your attic, which, by the way, needs serious cleaning? Can we please go downstairs now? All this dirt is a little much for me. I might start sweeping at any minute now."

"Yeah, sure, let's go before you decide to clean my attic," I chuckled.

This was so like her. She was always telling me to start cleaning more often. But I didn't care. I lived alone, and I cleaned as much as I needed to.

"So, what's up? I didn't know you were coming over," I said as we walked towards the stairs.

"I wasn't, and then I did," she said, "Actually, I had a bad feeling for some reason and needed a friend."

"Is everything okay?" I asked, worried that something might be wrong.

"Peachy," she said with a forced smile, "I know you will tell me that I'm being paranoid, but I couldn't stop thinking about you."

That was weird but not the answer I had feared. "Umm… Okay? And thinking about me is paranoia?" I didn't understand what she was getting at.

"Yes, because these thoughts aren't exactly the fun kind," she looked at me, "You're okay, right? You don't have any terminal illness or anything?"

"What?" Now, I laughed out loud. "What are you talking about? I'm perfectly fine. Why would you even ask that?"

"It's just a feeling I had, and then I thought I'd talk to you first before coming to my own conclusions." She was looking at me as if I was going to drop dead at any minute.

"Did you have a bad dream?" I was concerned because I knew that she took her dreams way too seriously.

"Sort of," she still looked worried. "Except I wasn't sleeping, so I don't know if we can call it a dream. More of a vision, you can say."

"A vision? You mean as in a glimpse into the future?" I was sure I looked astounded because that's how I felt. Since when did my cool, calm, and collected friend start having visions?

"I know, I know," she said exasperated. "It sounds weird to my ears too. But what can I do? I just had this vision, a feeling... Whatever you want to call it, and I had to come to find you."

I saw that she was shaken up, and whatever went on in her head drove her crazy.

"It's okay, don't worry. I'm here. I'm fine. You found me," I told her, trying to calm her down. We needed to get to the bottom of this, but I also needed my friend to think clearly before we spoke more on the subject.

"Sorry about that," she said, taking a deep breath, "it's probably nothing."

"Tell me everything," I encouraged her.

That's when she told me more about the feeling she had. She thought that I was in some danger. I played dumb. I let her think that her fears were unfounded. I said all the right things that I knew would calm her down. I didn't want my best friend, the only person outside of my immediate family that I loved, to worry about me dying.

It was going to happen soon. But it didn't mean I

would let people around me live in fear. I didn't plan to tell anyone. In all honesty, no one was going to believe me anyway.

Mahreen would, though. Even if she didn't have her encounter with the vision, she still would've believed me if I told her. That's how well we knew each other. We knew when one was hiding something because we knew all about each other— all there was to know.

"I'm feeling much better after talking to you," she sighed in relief, "I was being silly."

"Hey, it's okay," I said, "but now that you are here, how about we watch a movie and order in? I could use some company."

"Are you sure?" She looked doubtful. "You have nothing else planned?"

"You know I don't do plans. I can clean my attic any other day. I'm taking some time off from work. I told you, right?"

"Oh, yeah, you did. Why though? You never told me that?" she asked.

"I just need some time off. I'm going to figure out what I want to do next." I explained without giving away my real reason for it.

"Hmm... Well, I hope you finally do that," she teased me. She always said my life needed direction. Now, I just needed life, more of it, as much as I could get.

I know that she knows. I can see it in her eyes. Don't ask me how because I don't even know how I know, let alone how she does. We just do. I know I will die soon, and so does Mahreen. She confessed, and I lied to her. I told her she was being silly and that there was no way anyone could know when death would strike. I don't want her to think about my death. Hell, I don't want to think about it either. I hope that when the time comes, it takes us by surprise because we can't keep thinking about it. It's pointless. In the few months I have left, I plan to live my life to the fullest. I have a bucket list. And I'm going to do those things that I never had time for before now. The only thing I cannot do is let her know that I know.

∞∞∞∞

That was the day it started. Mahir's was the first death I saw. I just looked at him, and I knew when he would die, and it was soon. I wanted to tell him so badly, but there was no way I would worry him like that. I knew that he would believe me. That's how well he knew me. It would only mean that he would worry about it. I didn't want that. I could never worry him like that. In the end, I did tell him.

I couldn't sit still and do nothing. How could I let my friend die without at least trying to save his life? The only problem was that I had no idea how he would die. I knew when but not how or where. And without that knowledge, there was nothing I could do. I needed a plan, and I would formulate one that wouldn't fail me. Little did I know that planning was of no use when one was up against death.

$$\infty\infty\infty$$

"What are you doing up so late?" Mahir asked as soon as I picked up the phone.

"If you thought I was sleeping, why did you call?" I asked him, pretending to be annoyed.

"I wanted to talk to you, but I fully expected my call to go to the voice message." He tried to explain.

He shouldn't have bothered. There was nothing to explain. We could call each other any time, and we often did it at odd times, like when I was in a meeting or when he was out somewhere trying to find his next adventure.

I never understood what compelled him to get into extreme sports. He never liked it up until a few months ago. He just gave up his job and started mountain climbing, skiing, and whatnot. I sometimes wondered if my telling him about my vision was a bad idea. Maybe he thought that he was going to die soon, so why not live on the edge?

We, humans, are strange that way. You never know how anyone's going to react to something.

"Okay, so now that we've established that I'm awake, what do you want to talk to me about at this hour of the night?" I said.

"I just wanted to hear your voice before going to bed," he said, and that was probably the weirdest thing he had ever said to me.

"Why?" I was confused and wondered if there was something he wasn't letting on.

"No reason," he said, "do I need a reason to hear my best friend's voice?"

"No, that's not what I mean. You never do that, that's why I wondered. Anyway, forget it, and let's talk for as long as you like."

It wasn't anything important. We just talked shop and went to bed, like any other night. We had no idea that only one of us would be able to see the next day. Mahir died in his sleep. It happened, and he was gone without an apparent reason, and they said he died peacefully. It was just his time.

How could I have forgotten about that? It was so stupid. A few months ago, all I worried about was finding a death cure. I knew he would die in December, and when the time came, I didn't even realize it. I thought it was like any other night. We talked about silly, stupid things, and all the while, my friend was preparing to leave this plane of existence.

We grew up together, you know. Since the day we were kids, we did everything together. Somehow, we managed to stay friends throughout our lives. And his wasn't a long life, unfortunately. That was when we parted ways.

∞∞∞

My best friend is gone, and I'm left with this burden, and it's driving me crazy. Every time I look at someone, I know exactly when that person will die. The exact date of their demise suddenly appears on a wall in my head. I am not sure why I see it, but there it is. The only person whose death date I don't know is me. And there have been quite a few deaths to prove me right, so it's not like I can doubt it anymore, which makes it difficult for me to look people in the eye and talk about mundane things. It makes life too hard. What am I supposed to do with this knowledge? Should I even do something about it? These are the questions that plague my life, the thoughts that haunt my nights, and the fear that follows me all day long.

But death, I don't fear.

A Life Worth Living

All my life, I have felt like an outsider. No matter where I am or with whom, I don't fit in. I'm that weird kid, that strange girl, and that crazy woman. I have never felt like I belong somewhere or with someone. It's not that I don't have people in my life who love me. Rather their love isn't enough to make me feel at home. There's a restlessness in my soul I can neither explain nor shake it off.

I don't want to live this ordinary life. It doesn't seem like enough. You are born and go through different stages of life only to die one day. Poof! like that, you are no more. Sometimes you leave behind people who mourn you, while sometimes even that doesn't happen. Does it make any sense to you? Do you think that it's enough? Well, I don't. I don't want this life. This mundane existence, in my opinion, is completely worthless.

I wonder if I feel like this because I'm not happy with my life. And then, I wonder what is happiness anyway? Isn't it a state of mind, so rare and overrated at the same time? Or maybe it's my point of view that is twisted. Do you think I'm insane? If you do, I won't disagree with you because, in all honesty, I may very well be. Maybe we are all insane and sanity is just a myth.

If you ever find time to yourself, sit by a window with a cup of tea or coffee (whichever you prefer) and think about it, how superficial our lives are. We measure happiness with material things and sometimes with love. If someone loves you and you love them back, you start imagining yourself to be a happy person. That's all? Are we born just to find love? Why is it so important?

I find it strange that we all follow the same rules in life. Like sheep, we are all doing the same things, over and over again, until it all ends. But what if it never ends? What if you are reborn just to do the same silly things? How limited our knowledge of this existence is. However, there's a limit to our imagination, even though at times that doesn't seem to be the case.

Oh well, what am I talking about? I wonder how the story of my life turned out to be a series of questions that can never be answered adequately. I should better stop here or this monologue will never end.

So, where was I? Ah, yes, my inability to fit in. How strange it is. After all, I was born here like everyone else, and yet somehow, it feels all wrong. This world is not my world, as if I don't belong here, with other humans. At times, I feel like an alien. Maybe I am an alien who somehow got abandoned on this strange planet, and now she doesn't know how to get back home.

I wonder where home is? I hope it's someplace nice.

Someplace paradise-y, so to speak. How cool would that be? Don't you think? Anyway, let's start with the story and leave all the wondering for later. We will have plenty of time for that.

I read it, once, twice, and then deleted the whole thing. It was too soon to reveal the truth.

"Hey, what are you doing?"

I heard someone say and looked over my shoulder. It was my roommate, Sana. I thought she was out. Next time, I'd have to be more careful with when I choose to write. I couldn't let her read any of it. Composing myself and subtly closing my diary, I said, "Nothing much. You may say I'm woolgathering."

"When are you not." She smiled and sat down on a chair beside my bed. "So, if you aren't busy can we talk?"

"Sure." Glad that she didn't notice the diary or ask any questions about it, I gave her my full attention.

"I need help," she said as if doubting I'd help her.

"Okay," I said, prompting her to continue. Her doubt wasn't unfounded. I didn't want to commit to anything before knowing the details.

"Don't look so worried." She must have gauged my reluctance as she said, "I only need to borrow that book you were reading."

"Which one?" I was relieved to hear it was a

simple case of borrowing a book and not burying a dead body. Because when it was Sana, anything was possible.

"The one about soul searching. I hope to find something in it that might help me write my essay. It's due tomorrow," she said with a sigh.

"You always put off work until the last moment," I said, but couldn't help smiling. "Anyway, it's on the shelf there, and you can borrow it for as long as you like."

It was a book I found in an old bookshop a while ago. I had never heard of the author before, but it had such an inspiring cover that I bought it. I loved books. They were my only solace in this world. And old books were the best. I always felt they had more than one story to tell.

Lately, I read a lot about soul searching. Souls, I came to realize, were a unique thing, and I believed they were the reason humans were better than all other creations.

"Thanks for this." Sana was now holding the book. "I'll see you tomorrow in class."

I noticed her smile didn't reach her eyes, which was odd. With some concern, I asked, "Where are you going?"

"To the library, and then, to Sam's house. We plan to do a group study, and I know you hate those. That's why I didn't ask you," she said, shrugging.

The explanation was unnecessary as I didn't

mind not being included in anyone's social plans. "That's ok, I have a lot to do, anyway."

"Then carry on, you'll have the room to yourself." She waved over her head and left the room without a backward glance.

I was alone, once again. There was something I desperately needed to tell someone, but I didn't know how. The truth about me and my life. Soon, I hoped, I might get a chance to tell my story.

∞∞∞

"How did your group study go yesterday?" I asked Sana the next day when we were together in our room.

"It was good," she replied. "We worked and also enjoyed talking to each other. That's why I love to study with friends. It makes hard tasks more fun than they can ever be."

I smiled politely but said nothing as I didn't enjoy the company. The very idea of the group studies was uncomfortable for me. I liked to be alone as much as possible. It was bad enough that I had to share a room with Sana. But I was getting used to her. She was the only person I could tolerate for more than a few hours. Other than that, I preferred to keep to myself and read for pleasure when I wasn't studying for exams.

"So, about that book," she began to say something and then paused.

I waited, but when she didn't continue, I nudged her, "What about it?"

"Have you read it?" she said, biting her lips and looking anywhere but at me.

Wondering whether it was discomfort or worry I detected in her tone, I said, "I'm reading it, but no, I haven't read it to the end. Why?" I raised my eyebrows in curiosity.

"It's strange. I thought it was about metaphoric soul searching, but it talks about souls as if they can be seen and found outside of the human body." She finally looked at me, reading my expression closely to judge my reaction.

"And that's strange?" I was confused by her question and felt no need to censor my reaction.

"You don't think so?" Now, she sounded shocked and her eyebrows almost touched her hairline.

With a shrug, I said, "Not at all. Souls are just like flesh and blood. If you look closely, you can even see them."

"Okay." She probably didn't know how to respond to my claim, and I didn't know why I said it.

Humans couldn't see souls. But that was the problem, you see. The thing was that I wasn't human, and I saw souls all the time. They were a part of everyone and if I concentrated, they were visible to me. Sometimes, I didn't even have to look too closely.

"I'm kidding," I said, faking a laugh. I thought it better to deflect or she might start asking questions I wasn't yet willing to answer. There was no point in revealing something I knew she wouldn't understand. "I don't know. I'll have to read it to the end, but maybe the author was writing fiction while trying to be original. In any case, it's a good book. So far, I'm enjoying reading it."

"Yeah, it does sound like fiction," she said with a chuckle. "You had me worried there for a minute. Seeing souls?" She outright laughed then, but I said nothing.

I saw her soul. It was pure and full of life. She had one of the best souls I had seen on this planet. Most people had dark souls; some were as black as the moonless and starless night. I guess, the more you sinned the blacker it got. Not that I knew for sure. It was just a feeling I had—an understanding that came from within me.

"Are you going home during the spring break?" she asked, changing the subject.

"I don't know," I said, honestly. "Maybe, but it's not a good time for me to go home."

"Why?"

"It's a busy time for my parents. I'll be in their way." I didn't like talking about my family and hoped she would take the hint, but no such luck.

"I've never met your parents," she said.

"Oh, yeah?"

"I was hoping to meet them now," she smiled, "It would be great, don't you think?"

I got the impression she wanted me to invite her to stay with my parents and me, over the break. I wondered what was that all about, but I didn't say anything. I hated prying into other people's lives. If she wanted to share something with me, she would.

∞∞∞

As it turned out, my parents called me home, and I went. I hadn't gone back in a long time, and Since I wasn't expecting to, the unexpected change in plans filled me with excitement. I didn't invite Sana, though. Because it felt strange to take someone home with me. As I mentioned before, we weren't that close and I had never invited anyone to my family house. I assumed she'd visit her parents and probably had a better holiday than me.

Then, the strangest thing happened. Okay, probably not the strangest. But it was quite odd. When I came back after the break, Sana was nowhere to be found. She had vanished into the thin air.

She never went home, but she wasn't on campus either. No one knew what happened. One day she was there and the next she wasn't. I wasn't assigned a new roommate, because it was the middle of the semester and everyone already had rooms. Now, I was all alone. I should've been happy but I wasn't.

The truth was that I missed her. I never thought I would or could. I was always happy with a book. I rarely spent time with her outside of our room, yet I missed her. She had become a part of my life without me realizing it.

I wondered how she would've felt if I told her about myself. If she knew the truth, would she have been scared of me? Or perhaps fascinated? I wanted to find her, but I didn't know how.

Until I got an idea. It was time to tell my story. At last, I was ready. Besides, it was important for people to know me before they could understand how I found Sana when no one else could.

As I was saying, it was time to tell the truth that I was indeed an alien. *That* feeling I had was real. I was abandoned on earth without any clue. On one stormy night, my parents found me on their doorstep. They raised me and never told me that I wasn't their biological daughter. But I had a feeling I didn't belong. I couldn't fit into this world because I wasn't of it.

I found that out on my eighteenth birthday when I started seeing people's souls. I realized that not only could I see other people's souls, but I didn't have one. I was soulless. That was my first clue to finding my true identity.

What made it clearer were my dreams. I saw my real parents and I saw who I truly was. It was scary in the beginning, but soon, I accepted my identity. It wasn't a big deal. The universe was filled with secrets beyond our comprehension. What if I wasn't human? I was okay, and my life only got better after knew the truth about myself.

As I was saying, I could see souls. It wasn't difficult for me to look for Sana's soul. Hers was beautiful. I had always loved it. And when I looked for it, I found it. Unfortunately, it was without a body. Her body had died and her soul was left behind. She couldn't crossover into the otherworld, because she was sad and angry.

"How long are you planning to mourn your death?" I asked one day, but she didn't reply, of course. Souls couldn't talk. At least, not in the way I could understand. I was hoping that soon she would move on, but it had been months and she was still there. I wanted to know why, but I didn't know where to look for the answers. Then, it came to me.

"Zainy, wait up," Sam called out.

"Hello." I stopped in my tracks and looked at her coming toward me.

"I haven't seen you in a while," she said. "Where have you been?"

"I have been busy with study and work. You know how it is. Not much time for socializing."

"That may be," she continued, "but you should find time for friends. Or one day, you'd be left alone."

"I know, and I'll try." I agreed with her, but the truth was I would rather be alone with a book than be with people who never showed their true faces. I noticed something odd. Her soul was completely black now. It wasn't like that before. I wondered what had she done to cause this darkness in her soul.

"Anyhow," she gave me a broad smile, and said, "I was wondering if it's okay for me to hang out with you today. We can study or talk, whatever. What do you think?"

"Hmm." I wasn't so sure about spending time with her, but I also wanted to know more about what she was up to. "Sure, why not?"

"Cool, I'll come around seven?"

"Sure, see you."

Later that night she came over to my room. Sana's soul was there too and wasn't happy about it. I saw the changes. It was as if her soul was scared of Sam's. That revelation gave me a pause. I desperately wanted to know what was wrong with it. And somehow, I figured it out.

I wasn't entirely sure how, but one minute I was wondering about it, and the answer came to me.

Sam had killed Sana. It was strange how I knew it, but in my mind, there was no doubt about it.

Both of their souls showed me the truth. It was like the souls talked and I listened. That had never happened before. Still, it wasn't farfetched considering I was an alien no one knew about.

"Were you and Sana close?"

Her question brought me back from my musings. "Yes, you can say that. At least, I like to think we were."

"Did she ever tell you anything interesting before she went missing?" she asked guardedly.

I had no idea what she wanted to know. Yes, Sana and I were close in our way. But no, we didn't use to have many heart-to-hearts. I wasn't that kind of person. I liked to keep my distance even from the person I called a friend.

"Like what?" I said.

"Oh, you know, just this and that." She was being deliberately vague.

"I don't know, we talked about a lot of things. You'll have to be more specific."

"Oh, forget it," she said with a weird smile. "I just wondered what her last days were like and what she might've talked about. You know, that kind of thing."

I noted how she had said 'her last days' as if she knew Sana was dead and not coming back. "Sorry,

I can't think of anything in particular that might interest you," I said.

"It's okay, no need to apologize. I was so close to her. You know how much time we used to spend together. I miss her so much."

She was lying and I knew it. Her soul was getting darker and darker the more she talked. She was up to something, and it was nothing good.

"We were working on an article together," she continued, "did she tell you about it?"

"An article?" I was genuinely confused. "About what? Why?"

"Oh, well, it was my idea. I was working on something for our newspaper and asked for her help."

"I had no idea." And I really didn't know anything about it. "Was it something important?"

"Don't worry about it. I don't know why I brought it up," she said, changing the subject as soon as she realized I didn't know anything about any article. "How is your work going?"

"Not bad," I shrugged. "Hey, you know I just remember, I need to work on my essay for tomorrow's class. Do you mind? I'm sorry, but I don't have time to continue this."

"No problem, I was leaving anyway." She said goodbye and left.

It was a strange encounter, to say the least. I

wasn't friends with Sam at all. I barely knew her and yet, she wanted to spend time with me. And then, she asked me questions about Sana, which sounded a lot like an interrogation to me.

It was then that I remembered Sana's journal. The one she used to write in all the time. I knew where it was. For some reason, she always kept it with my books instead of her own. Maybe that would give me the answers I wanted badly.

I wish I had known about it before I got involved with Sam. She lied to me. She isn't who she says she is. I wonder if she's even human. I don't know what to do with this knowledge. I can't go to the police. They will never believe me. I can hardly believe it myself. If I hadn't seen it with my eyes, I would never have believed it. She is a monster. And I'm scared of her.

It all started when she asked me to borrow Zainy's book. I hadn't even noticed that book before, but Sam knew about it. She had seen Zainy reading it in the cafe once. Long story short, I borrowed it for her. She told me not to tell Zainy. And I didn't.

I only skimmed through it myself to know what it was about. It didn't seem interesting to me. All that soul talk. Honestly, I didn't understand it much. In any case, I gave it to Sam. She was excited about it for some reason and kept thanking me. I had no idea what was going on.

Only if I had known, I'd never have let her read that book. I would have burned the book myself. It was a terrible fate that befell so many people because of that one book.

I'm going to expose her before more people get hurt. I'll write about it and tell the story to the world. She's pure evil. She needs to be locked away. The world needs to be saved.

I have returned the book to Zainy for now. I hope she doesn't know its true nature. I'll burn it the first chance I can get. No one else should find it. No one must use it the way Sam did. I will make sure of that.

It was the last entry in her journal. I couldn't make any sense of it. The first thing I did was to look for the book. I realized it was nowhere to be found. So, Sana did burn it in the end. I wondered what Sam did with the book that spooked her and made her sound like a crazy woman when she wrote about it in her journal.

One thing was clear to me, I needed to find answers no matter what. I couldn't rest until I knew what was happening. Why had Sam killed Sana? And what else had she done to be called *'pure evil'* by my friend, who herself didn't have a single evil bone in her body?

Soon, I got all the answers I needed. Although, they weren't what I wanted to know. Sometimes, I even wish that I had left the matter alone, turned a blind eye, anything to keep me from learning the truth about Sam, and about so much more.

∞∞∞

"Hey," It was Sam again, "do you have a minute?"

"Sure thing," I said, trying to keep my smile genuine. "What's it about this time?"

"Oh," she said, "nothing much, I was just hoping to borrow your copy of the Soul Seers again. You know, the book you lent to Sana before. I didn't get to read the whole book, so I was hoping to do it now. It's very interesting."

"I'm sorry, but I seem to have lost it. Maybe Sana never returned it. I don't exactly remember. You can try finding it in the library."

"No problem. I'll try somewhere else." She gave me a strange smile and left without saying anything else.

I wondered why she was looking for the book again. Good thing Sana burnt it, who knew what that book was all about? Now that I thought about it, the book did mention people like me, people who could see souls, among a lot of other things related to souls. I had only read the first few chapters of the book, and I wished I had read it all. Maybe then I would've gotten the answers I wanted.

"Hey, Zainy wait up," Sara was calling my name. "Did you hear the news?"

"What news?"

"Let's go to your room and talk for a while."

We walked together in silence. When we entered my room, I asked her again about the news she was talking about.

"Oh, it's kind of sad. They've found a body. Everyone thinks it's Sana."

It may have been news to people who were hoping Sana was still alive. I knew better, though. I had already seen her bodiless soul.

"That's just…" I didn't know what to say.

"Yeah, I know you two were close. As close as you can be with anyone, that is."

Sara's soul was a unique yellow color that I hadn't noticed before. But then I didn't always look for people's souls. Sara wasn't close to me or Sana. She was just a fellow student. We weren't even in the same classes. I had seen her around and I knew she hung out with Sam's group sometimes. It was odd that she knew me enough to make that last remark.

"Yes, she was my closest friend. I hope they find her killer soon," I said distractedly.

"So, you think she was killed?" Sara looked at me with curiosity.

"Well, who else would bury her body?" I stated the obvious.

"That's a valid question. We all hoped she had run away or something. This is just unbelievable. Who would do such a thing? Sana was such a kind person, and everyone loved her."

I knew people often said things like that about the dead. Though, in Sana's case, it was the truth. She was loved by all. That was the kind of girl she was—loving and caring. I felt her loss acutely at that moment. The world had lost the nicest humans and the purest soul. I could attest to that.

"Do you mind, I want to be alone right now," I said.

"Oh, sure. I don't mind it at all. I can understand." With that Sara left. She understood my need to be alone.

I wasn't alone, though. Sana's soul was with me. She was still there, and now, I knew why she was unable to crossover. She needed justice and I was going to get it for her, even if it cost me my life.

I knew where her parents lived and I decided to visit them. It was a natural thing to do as they were holding her funeral in a few days and I was her roommate.

"I'm sorry I didn't come earlier. I should've visited sooner. I'm so sorry," I said, wishing there was something I could do for them, but all I had was my words.

"It's okay, dear. I know you were close to Sana. She used to talk about you all the time. We hoped she was safe somewhere. She had her problems, but we never thought she could be gone like this." Her mom was having a hard time coping with her death. "You can stay in her room until the funeral. I'm sure she wouldn't have minded it. She was such a private girl, but you were her favorite person in the world."

"I had no idea." I was taken aback at the affection her mother was showing me. Now, I knew where Sana got her loving personality. But to think she talked about me to her family warmed my heart.

"Oh yes, she practically worshiped you. Just this morning, when I was going through her things, I found a letter and a box labeled "for Zainy." She left those things for you. I didn't open it because I know you girls need your secrets," she said with a sad smile. "It's in her room. You can look at it anytime you want."

"That's so thoughtful of you, but I really can't impose. I have booked myself a room in a hotel. I'll be fine there."

"It won't be an imposition. We'd love to have you in the house, even if for a few days. You remind me of her so much," she was teary-eyed again. Dabbing at her eyes, she said, "I'm sorry dear, do excuse me."

"I'll stay if that's make you happy." And that was

settled then.

After dinner, I went to her room. Sleep was nowhere in my near future, and I decided to see what Sana had left for me. I opened the letter first.

Dear Zainy,

If you are reading this, then I'm probably not in this world anymore. Unfortunately, I have stumbled upon a secret that's going to cost me my life. I hope I'm able to reveal it to the world before I die, but if I'm unable to do so, then I want to share it with you, at least. Because you are the only person I can think of.

You may think me crazy after reading this and going through the box, but I assure you I am not. This is all true. Oh, how I wish it weren't! Zainy, be careful, though. Some people in this world are not what they seem to be. Sam is one of those. She is evil. You must warn the world before it's too late.

I have gathered as much information as I could. I don't know the whole story, but I know enough. I plan to publish an article about it in our newspaper and hope someone will pay attention and take it seriously. I will also report it to the authorities, even if I'm locked up in a mental institution. I don't care. Such evil must be exposed before it's too late.

Do you remember that book I borrowed from you? It's not fiction. It's all true. I've seen the proof of it. Souls are real and people who can see them are also real. But what's more shocking is that there are people who can steal souls. When they kill someone in a certain way, they can absorb the soul of the dying person. That makes them invincible.

I don't know their end goal. My research didn't go that far. I know that Sam is one of them. That book wasn't about metaphoric soul searching. It was about literal soul searching. Sam is going to kill hundreds of people to steal their souls. We must stop her and people like her before they do something disastrous.

You have to believe me. If I'm gone, then you must reveal the truth. I hope you don't discard this letter as ramblings of a mad woman and take me seriously.

Yours forever,

Sana.

I believed her. I didn't need much convincing, considering that I wasn't even human and also, knowing that souls had many purposes. It wasn't beyond belief that someone would find a way to steal and use souls for their selfish gains. But I wondered about killing hundreds of people.

What did Sana mean? How would Sam do that without detection? Killing one or two people was something else, but killing hundreds? Maybe I would find more evidence in the box she left for me.

As I opened the box, I found that my book was in it. My assumption that Sana must have burnt it was wrong. There were a whole bunch of papers and pictures beside it. It was impossible to go through everything in one night, but I had time. I spent the days before her funeral going through everything that was there. Now, I knew more than I ever had.

∞ ∞ ∞

The day of her funeral was as gloomy as any day could be. It had been raining since dawn. The sky was darker than it was normal during the summer months. We were all sad.

Sana's parents hadn't been able to stop crying. There were a lot of people attending the funeral; friends, family, and acquaintances. Seeing so many familiar and unfamiliar faces made me realize how much Sana was loved. Everyone missed her. The brightest person in the world, she was like a star that shone from within.

Sam was there too. That evil witch and the hypocrite. I hated that she could come to her funeral after killing her in cold blood.

"I hear you've been staying with Sana's parents," she said to me.

"That's right. But I can't talk to you right now. I've too much on my mind." I didn't bother to be polite to her today and left her standing there, probably wondering what was up with me.

I couldn't stand her knowing that she was the killer. Her black obsidian soul was on display and it didn't have to concentrate to see it. And once again, I couldn't help but notice how different it was from other souls; somehow more powerful—more pronounced. I hated what she was. But today was not for her. It was for Sana, and I would deal with Sam later. For now, I had to send my sweet friend off to the otherworld, in peace.

"Now if anyone would like to say a few words please go ahead."

I stood up. It was time to read the eulogy and hope that my friend could move on to where she was supposed to be.

Some of you may know me, but most of you don't. My name is Zainy and I was Sana's roommate and her friend. She was the closest person I had in my life and she was the kindest soul I ever saw. As you already know. We would miss her, no doubt. Losing her so suddenly has caused a rift in many of our lives. I just hope that wherever she is now, she is happy. May her soul rest in peace.

She was there I knew it. Her soul had been with me this whole time. I wished she would find the strength to leave this world behind. She needed my helping hand and I was going to lend it to her. This was the least I could do for my only friend.

Her soul was so pure. I know that for her there is only heaven. It's time for her soul to leave this plane. It may not be easy, but it's the only thing remaining for her to do.

I looked toward her soul as I said these words. I knew she was listening to me. I hoped this would work. I wanted to see her soul enter the bliss promised to the pure-hearted.

You must leave now. It is time. I know that it seems scary and I know that you're angry. You can trust me. I would do what you could not. You don't have to stay here anymore.

Everyone was looking at me as if I had gone crazy, but I didn't care. I had to convince Sana to leave. Because I knew the longer she stayed on Earth the harder it would become for her to leave. And souls that get permanently stuck here lose their sanity. They become trapped. And who knew what happened to them after that?

I couldn't risk my friend losing her chance at happily ever after. That was what she had in store, without a doubt. She was going to heaven and I wanted to make sure that she did, as soon as possible.

Von ma te lla en sig le lam etala

That was the spell to open the door to the otherworld, that I found in my book. Only Sana and I could see the door opening. Everyone else just thought I was rambling gibberish. Seeing my friend's soul leaving was worth the scorn from people around me.

I didn't stay after that. I left the funeral home, packed my things, and went back to my dorm room.

I knew Sam would realize that I had used the spell. Since she wasn't a soul seer, she wouldn't have been able to see the door or Sana's soul leaving. But she knew enough about the book and its magic to know what I had done. I had to prepare for what was coming next and there was no time to waste.

At last, I was ready. It was time to tell my story and also solve the mystery revolving around Sana's death. How strange to know that the two things were connected. I knew many people wouldn't believe it, but that was not important.

It didn't matter, because telling my story wasn't what was going to stop Sam. It was just about getting the truth out whether someone believed it or not. For Sam, I had something entirely different in mind.

$\infty \infty \infty$

Sam opened the door as soon as I rang the bell. "Hey, Zainy, what a pleasant surprise," she said with a fake smile. "Do come in."

"Thanks, I hope it's not a bad time. I need to talk to you."

"Not at all. It's the perfect time because I also want to talk to you about something." She led me to the living room.

"Really?" I feigned ignorance just to annoy her.

"Yeah, I think it was beautiful what you said at the funeral, but it kind of made me feel bad." She said as soon as I took a seat.

"Why would it make you feel bad?" Tilting my head, I scrutinized her.

"Well, you see, it made me realize what a liar you are." The irony of her statement wasn't lost on me.

"And why would I lie to you?" I said, smiling.

"I know you read that book. You can tell me now." Menace seeped into her tone, and I knew she was done pretending.

"Oh that," I said and shrugged. "Well, I hadn't read it when you asked me last time. But yes, I have read it now. I don't see any reason to lie about it. It's a great book."

"Then you understand it?" She looked shocked.

"Perfectly." I was amused.

"So, why are you here?" She sounded confused.

"I know what you are, and I'm going to stop you," I stated plainly.

"How are you going to manage that?" She had a cunning smile on her face. Her true face was on display, and she was underestimating me until the very end.

"You shall see very soon," I said.

"*Frey la de lam keri mehmo*," she chanted.

"It won't work on me." I smiled broadly. "You can't kill me. You see, I've got a secret of my own."

"How is this possible?" She was beyond shocked and fearful.

"It's very much possible you filthy Soul Seeker," I said. "I'm afraid I don't have a soul for you to collect."

"No, that's ... impossible!"

"It's not, as you can see." I was pleased to see her shaking with fear.

"What do you want?" she asked, changing her demeanor.

"I'm going to strip you of your power. *Cata mafi le da em ka*." As soon as I chanted the spell, Sam fainted. Her powers were gone and she could no longer collect souls. Next time when she regained her consciousness, she would be as normal as any other human being.

After I read Sana's notes, I did some research of my own. Sam was a witch and a descendant of a powerful clan of witches. They harnessed souls to draw their magic from.

I was an alien without a soul. Only I could strip her power from her. Her magic worked by affecting the soul. My not having a soul made me immune to her tricks. I now knew why I was sent to this world. My mission was to cleanse the human world of soul seekers. They were witches who only brought pain to the planet.

Sam was going to cast a spell that would have caused a massive tornado, thus killing hundreds of people. While she would've been waiting to harness their souls. If she had succeeded it would've made her unstoppable.

Good thing that Sana warned me. I stopped her in time, but my work was far from done. In fact, it had only just begun. There were witches in the world who needed to be brought to justice like Sam. It was true that she couldn't be punished for witchcraft. At least, not by the law. But for a witch, losing her powers was the worst punishment.

However, Sana's murder demanded justice as well. So, I had to find a way to prove that Sam killed her. With a little bit of magic of my own and some luck, it wasn't that difficult. I was able to confirm that Sam was the last person Sana saw, and from there, it was easy to find enough clues to get her convicted. Police did the rest, and now Sam was behind bars where she belonged. I hoped Sana's soul could now rest in peace without regrets or resentment.

My story was told, at last. And people knew all about witches and me. It also made my job a little easier as many arrogant witches had the audacity to confront me. They all got what they deserved, and the rest of them wouldn't be far behind.

I was no longer a loner. I was also a witch hunter. The world needed me, and I needed a purpose to live. In the end, we all got what we wanted the most.

Did I mention that I am immortal? Yep, one of the perks of being soulless. This was it for me, a life that would go on forever.

But I got to tell you, it was a life worth living.

Acknowledgements

There are so many people I would like to thank, without whom this collection wouldn't have been possible. First of all, I want to thank my mother for cheering me on. She is my biggest supporter, and I owe a lot to her. Secondly, I want to thank the online community, my fellow authors, and readers who have taken the time to read my work and provided me with helpful pointers to improve it. Last but not least, I want to thank my muse, who showed up every time I needed him. Without them, this collection would have stayed a dream and nothing more. So, thank you, everyone!

About the Author

Dr. Fizza Younis resides in the vibrant city of Lahore, Pakistan, where her journey through life has been as diverse as the tapestry of her country. With a Ph.D. in economics, she has delved deep into the intricate webs of financial theory, but it's the enchanting realms of fiction and poetry that have captured her heart. As a dedicated indie author and ardent reader, she revels in the art of storytelling, crafting narratives that transcend the boundaries of her academic pursuits. Rooted in the principles of minimalism, equality, and harmony, her writing reflects her steadfast beliefs. Her stories are both mirrors of her philosophy and windows into the lives of intriguing characters navigating the labyrinth of existence. In her world, characters come alive, and their misadventures resonate with the shared joys and tribulations of humanity. With every word, she sprinkles love and encouragement, creating a cocoon of empathy and connection that envelops her readers. Though she might describe herself as an average person leading a mundane existence, in the world of fiction, Fizza is nothing short of spectacular. Join her on a journey through the written word, where ordinary lives take on extraordinary hues, and the essence of humanity is distilled into every sentence.